RECKLESS FALL

SINFUL TRUTHS BOOK 3

ELLA MILES

FREE BOOKS

Read **Taken by Lies** for **FREE!** And sign up to get my latest releases, updates, and more goodies here→EllaMiles.com/freebooks

Follow me on **BookBub** to get notified of my new releases and recommendations here→Follow on BookBub Here

Join **Ella's Bellas FB group** to get **Pretend I'm Yours** for **FREE**→Join Ella's Bellas Here

TRUTH OR LIES WORLD

TRUTH OR LIES SERIES:

Taken by Lies #1
Betrayed by Truths #2
Trapped by Lies #3
Stolen by Truths #4
Possessed by Lies #5
Consumed by Truths #6

SINFUL TRUTHS SERIES:

Sinful Truth #1
Twisted Vow #2
Reckless Fall #3
Tangled Promise #4
Fallen Love #5
Broken Anchor #6

PROLOGUE

SIREN

The truth is a strange thing.

I've always been one who valued the truth. I always spoke it even if my actions or behaviors were less than one hundred percent true.

I've tried lying. Time and time again, but I can never get the words out, that's how important the truth is to me.

The day I started working for Julian Reed, the truth started to bend. My entire life became about working for a man I hated. I thought I was doing it for love. I thought I was protecting Hugo Martinez, a man I loved. A man I envisioned forever with.

But is it really love when it's one-sided? If the man you love doesn't love you back?

From the day Hugo betrayed me, I made a vow to myself to never love again. I told myself I didn't need love. I definitely didn't need a man in my life. I told myself I was a strong, independent woman. I owed no loyalty to him but was unable to sentence Hugo to death, which is what I would have done had I ended my vow to Julian. So I kept my promise to Julian to ensure that Hugo stayed alive. I think some small part of me hoped that my sacrifice would make Hugo fall in love with me again, even though I knew I would never accept his love. He didn't deserve to die for his betrayal. It's not Hugo's fault he fell in love with another woman.

Love is, after all, uncontrollable. If we could tame love, we would choose to only fall for those people who would make the best match for us. Ones in the same social circles, the same financial status. Ones our families approve of. We would only fall for the safe ones. Ones who only made us better instead of bringing out the worst in us.

But we don't get to choose who we fall for. We just fall...
Carelessly.
Whole-heartedly.
Recklessly.

For months now, I've told myself I'm not falling. I can't fall. I'm incapable of loving, not after being hurt so many times by men. I told myself that Zeke Kane was just like the rest of the men in my life. That he was as bad as all the rest. But at every turn, he proved me wrong. He saved me time and time again, at the expense of himself. He protected innocent women from being sold. He showed me that he cared—about his boss, his friends, his family, and even me. He could have loved me if I had let him.

But Zeke thinks I betrayed him, even when I didn't. He thinks I hurt him. And that's what I want him to think. It's the only way to save him. The only way for him to eventually get free. And now I have the perfect plan to get him out of this mess with Julian. A way to get him off the island.

I can save Zeke, earn my redemption in his eyes. There is just one problem...I've learned that I *can* lie, at least to one person—myself.

I've been lying for months. Telling myself I can't fall in

love, and I sure as hell can't fall for a dangerous man like Zeke. If I was going to fall, I should fall for a teacher or banker, not a man in this crime world.

The truth is, I did fall. My heart fell off a cliff the day I met him, and it's been falling a little more ever since. Until now, I'm so deep in love with him that I can't think straight. I can't breathe without inhaling Zeke's smell. I can't dream without Zeke in my head. I can't exist without him. *But I have to.*

Zeke may think I'm a selfish bastard, someone who has betrayed him time and time again. The truth is, I love him. I've always loved him. I've never betrayed him. I just can't tell him the truth.

1
———

SIREN

FALLING IN LOVE IS EASY; not getting hurt is the hard part. Not destroying the one you love—that's the hardest of all.

I stare down at the man lying in the hospital bed. My first love—Hugo Martinez. He looks so broken and shattered. His face is beaten up. Tubes connect to his arms. Bandages cover his body. And the gentle sound of a beep on the machine next to him is the only indication that he's still alive and not dead.

Hugo made me believe love is real. Sure, I'd thought I'd felt it before with my high school crush. When I fell in love with the stray dog in the neighborhood. When Nora became my best friend. And sure, that was love. But it's not the same as falling in love.

When I fell for Hugo, he became my everything. I couldn't think except of him. I couldn't plan my day without him in it. I couldn't breathe...

I became a little obsessed. *No, obsessed isn't the right word; I became enchanted with him.* Hugo could do no wrong in my eyes. He was it. The elusive one. I knew it from the moment he kept me from putting another needle in my arm and yanked me up off the street where I was planning on offering my body in exchange for money. Hugo saved me from a life of sin. He saved me from myself. If I had slept with a stranger for money, I wouldn't have survived. I would have never forgiven myself.

And then he kept saving me. From the drugs. The depression. The anger. He saved me from it all.

At twenty-one, he felt like a man, while I was barely eighteen and still acted like a child. Hugo helped me find who I was. Taught me self-defense. Bought me my first guitar. But then, he became so much more.

He taught me how to kiss. When his lips touched mine, fireworks exploding was an understatement.

When his fingers explored my body, toe-curling orgasms followed.

Hugo was my match. He made me a better person, and I was in desperate need of becoming a better person. I was desperate to have something to live for. And Hugo filled that void. He gave me more than something to live for; he gave me my life back.

I came alive against his lips.

I thrived in his arms.

And I learned to find purpose even when Hugo was gone.

Which became more and more often. I didn't realize Hugo was fighting his own battles while I was becoming stronger. I didn't realize he was making his own plans even while proposing forever with me.

I didn't realize that falling in love with Hugo meant giving him the ammunition he needed to kill me. He had the ability to wipe me from this earth with one blow—and he did.

After Hugo betrayed me, I became a different person.

One incapable of love. I gave it all to him. Married him. Sacrificed ten years of my life vowing to work for Julian in order to save his life.

And Hugo shit all over my love. He showed me not only how little he cared about my feelings, but that he enjoyed hurting me.

I tried to take my heart back. I tried to ease the pain in my chest. But I couldn't. I couldn't re-capture my heart.

It took me a while to get over the disloyalty, to be able to breathe again. And when I did, I wanted to take the vow back. Let Hugo deal with his own mess, even if it meant Julian or the drug lord Hugo owed money to would kill him.

But as much as I act heartless, as much as I want to punish bad men, I couldn't sentence Hugo to death. I tried. I've tried countless times over the last seven years when Julian ordered me to do something I didn't want to do. But I couldn't.

Call it love.

Call it heartbreak.

Call it loyalty.

Call it whatever you want. I feel like a coward every time I can't let Hugo go, but it's not just letting him go that holds me back. If I end my vow to Julian, I have no doubt that he would kill Hugo. Julian is the reason Hugo is in the hospital —to remind me what will happen if I break my vow.

I look at Hugo lying in the bed, lifeless. I could kill him. It would be so easy. Suffocate him with the pillow. Snap his neck. Unhook the tubes providing him life. Push too many narcotics through his IV.

I could end this. I could be free. At least of Hugo.

I stand over his bed, considering how easy it would be to kill the man who both gave me back my life and then ruined it.

But I can't kill him, because I'm not heartless. And Hugo still holds the tiniest piece. A piece that has turned cold, black, and unfeeling.

I look back to the hallway that Zeke escaped through. His words will haunt me forever. He won't protect me anymore. He won't save me; that was his vow.

Those may have been the words he spoke, but I know what he was really saying, *I won't love you anymore. I won't let my heart fall anymore.*

He may have never said I love you. But we were close, even though we shouldn't have been. We both tormented and betrayed each other time and time again. I did everything I could to make Zeke hate me. I claimed it's because I don't want to fall in love again. Thought I pushed him away only for selfish reasons—I don't want to give a man the power to hurt me again.

But it was a lie, maybe the first lie I ever told myself.

Because I didn't push Zeke away to save myself, I pushed Zeke away to save him. And he still fell for Julian's trap. Because Zeke isn't like Hugo, he's a man of honor. A loyal man. A man who loves with everything he has. A man capable of changing the world.

He doesn't deserve to be trapped in this life. He deserves to be free. To return to his friends. His boss. His life.

I'll be trapped here forever. I have three years left of my debt to Julian, but that isn't the only thing keeping me trapped, holding me hostage.

My heart clenches, looking at the empty hallway. Zeke is most likely headed back to Julian now, trying to find a way to get out of his own deal with him or figuring out how to complete it as fast as possible so he can get the hell away from me.

Hugo may hold a tiny piece of my heart I never got back, but Zeke holds the rest of my heart. It belongs to Zeke.

Because I fell...

Hard.

Stupidly.

In love with Zeke.

I fell too fast.

I fell too hard.

Long before I ever admitted it to myself. I tried to protect Zeke from my love by making him hate me. But it backfired on me.

I'm done hiding my love, but it's too late.

Zeke hates me.

Good. That means there is no reason to hide how I feel. He'll lash back and try to hurt me, and I'll let him. Because I deserve it. I failed to protect him from Julian. But I can set him free.

I look back at Hugo. I want him dead. But first, I want the tiny piece of my heart he still holds. It's not his. I want it back. I want to give Zeke Kane everything—my entire heart. Even though I know how much it will hurt when he doesn't love me back. Even though I know the pain when he betrays me. *Wrecks me.*

I want to feel it: the good and the bad. I want to show him how much I love him. I want to fall, screw the consequences. My life is no longer mine. But my heart, my heart is all that I have left to give. And if I'm going to give it up, I'm going to give it to a man like Zeke.

A man who, in a different life, I would have loved from the moment I laid eyes on him. I would have loved out in the open. We would have made each other better, instead of bringing out the worst in each other. Hating Zeke didn't save him, maybe loving him will.

"I hate you," I say.

"You sure about that? Because your puffy eyes and running nose say differently. You came running back to me as soon as you found out I was in the hospital," Hugo answers, without opening his eyes.

Did he really speak? Or am I imagining he did?

Either way, he's right. I did. I shouldn't have come back, though. And Hugo can't read me as well as he used to. Because this isn't love, this is heartbreak. And it's nothing compared to how I felt watching Zeke walk out the door.

2

———

ZEKE

SIREN'S FUCKING MARRIED. She's capable of love. She's not heartless. She can fall in love, just not with me.

She hurt me once, shame on her.

She hurt me twice, shame on me.

I won't let her hurt me a third time.

My heart may have been falling, but seeing her run to another man. Seeing her pain for a man who was hurt, that turned my heart to stone.

I will never let her in again. I will never love her. Never care for her. Never consider her on my side. I will never protect her again.

She betrayed me to Julian, and now she's married to another man. I don't care if she claims she doesn't love him. That he hurt her, and they just haven't gotten around to divorce. I don't care what her excuses are. I'm done.

Done with her. Done with my deal with Julian. I'm done.

I want out of here. I'll make sure Enzo, and Kai, and Langston, and Liesel are safe and protected by killing Julian. Then I'll destroy Siren, so I know she will never come after my family. I won't kill her, I'm not vicious enough to be able to finish the job, but I'll get my message across that if she comes for me, she's a dead woman.

I'm tired of playing games. I want answers. And I don't trust Siren. I want the truth. And the only way I'll get that is from Julian.

I drive fast toward Julian's house. Away from the hospital. Away from her—my siren. She will never be anything but a siren. The devil in disguise. The woman who told me who she was with one word. And I was too stupid to believe that she might be what she claimed—a monster.

I drive, imagining what Siren would say if she were riding next to me. How pissed off she would be that I'm driving too fast. I'm being reckless. I'm going to get into a car accident.

I smirk.

Good, let's see if she would come running to my bedside if I were to get into a car accident. I doubt it.

I press my foot down on the pedal harder as I turn a curve, the truck swerves, but I make the turn, barely avoiding rolling off the edge of the hill and down the cliffside. It doesn't slow me down, though. It only makes me drive faster, trying to outrun my pain.

Somehow I make it to Julian's drive without crashing. I throw my door open and jump out, slamming the door hard behind me—wishing I could hurt Siren the way I just hurt the door. But I can't hurt Siren, because she doesn't care about me. She just likes watching me bleed.

I pull my gun out of my pocket as I storm inside Julian's house. One of his servants spots me and turns on the spot, heading back down the hallway when he sees my gun. I'm going to finish what I should have done months ago. I'm going to kill Julian Reed. And then I'm getting the fuck off this island.

I march down the hallway, to Julian's office, the scent of cigar smoke leading the way. I kick open the door and aim my gun at his head.

I should fire immediately, kill him without questions. But I want answers. I need answers. I need closure, so when I leave, I won't have Siren floating around in my head, fucking with me.

Julian chuckles when he sees me standing in the doorway. Not the reaction I'm used to when I aim a gun at someone's head.

"I've been expecting you," he says, puffing casually on his cigar.

"Then, you know I'm here to get answers and then kill you."

He exhales. "I might be willing to give you some answers. But you won't be killing me."

I step into the room, keeping my gun trained at his head. "I will. Your little guard dog isn't here to protect you this time. You sent her away to take care of the man she loves."

Julian chuckles louder, until he's throwing his head back and his belly jiggles.

I fucking hate him.

"I also think it's hilarious that you are about to die," I say.

His dark eyes snap back to me. "I'm not about to die. But you have to admit, my Aria is good. She got you to fall for her, when she was married to another man the entire time."

"I didn't fall for her."

He lifts his scotch to his lips. "Then why did you save her? Why did you come storming over here threatening to kill me but not actually killing me?"

I don't answer him. I refuse to accept that I fell for her. *Sure, she's strong, independent, sassy, smart, kickass. But she's* also a liar, deceitful, selfish, and in love with another man. I'm better than falling for her tricks.

"Sit," Julian says.

I frown. *I'm not doing a damn thing this man asks again.*

"Sit, and I'll answer your questions."

"I don't—"

"Don't lie; the only reason I'm still breathing is because you have questions. Now fucking sit."

I refuse. I won't let anyone control me, not anymore. I want out of my deal, and as I see it, the best way to do that is by killing the man in front of me.

"You're just like Aria," Julian smiles to himself.

"I'm nothing like her. I'm loyal, honest, a good person."

"Unfortunately, she's all those things, too, even if she refuses to show you that side of herself."

I freeze. *Maybe I don't want Julian's point of view on things? He's just as manipulative as Siren is.*

I turn, planning on walking out and shooting him only as I leave.

"Aria can't divorce Hugo, that's why she hasn't."

His words cause me to stop. Because I want to know the truth. I need to know. I need to know everything. *What makes Siren tick? What makes her do what she does? What makes the strongest woman I know bow to such men?*

Love?

Hate?

I'm tired of being goaded. I'm tired of not fighting back. I turn and run with everything I have, knocking Julian out of the chair until he's on the floor on his back. I grab his neck and push him hard into the ground as I aim the gun at his head.

"Tell me everything, now."

His smile drops, but there is still light behind his eyes.

He still doesn't think this is his end. But from where I'm sitting, I know this is when Julian Reed dies.

"Why can't Siren divorce Hugo?" I ask.

"Because of the prenup she signed."

"What does the prenup say?"

"I don't know, but Hugo drunkenly told me one night that she is his forever because she signed a contract without reading it first. She trusted him, and now she's trapped. She would have to give up something she's not prepared to give up. You'll have to ask him or her what the prenup says."

I will.

"Does she still love him?" I ask, even though I know it's a stupid question. Julian doesn't know the answer. And even if he did, he's just going to manipulate me.

"Do you still love her even though she betrayed you?"

No. *Yes.*

"There is no *still*. I never fell for her. I hate her."

"Hate is the opposite of love. You can only truly hate those you once loved."

I push the gun against his head. "No, I hate you, and trust me, I never loved you."

Julian smiles. "You don't hate me like you hate her."

And then I hear her—Siren. She's standing in the doorway.

Fuck, I thought she'd still be at the hospital. What is she doing here?

I should have killed Julian, immediately. Now she's going to try and stop me like last time.

"You here to try and stop me from killing your boss?" I ask, staring at Julian, refusing to look at her.

"No. I'll finish my vow to Julian as long as he's breathing. I'll complete the tasks he's too chicken to carry out on his own. I'll put my life at risk every day facing his biggest enemies. But I'm done being his personal bodyguard. I re-read the contract I signed. There is nothing there saying I have to protect him at risk of my own life." Siren walks over to one of the chairs. She sits down and kicks her legs up on the coffee table and then puts her arms behind her head. "I'm just here for the show."

Siren isn't going to stop me from killing Julian. I'll have to deal with her when this is finished. I can't just let her go free. I don't trust her. She could continue Julian's mission of hunting down Enzo Black and his family. But right now, I'm focused on Julian.

"Any last words?" I ask, done with him.

Julian's eyes cut from me to Siren and then back again. If eyes could kill, his would have killed us both.

Finally, Julian is going to be dead. We are going to be free of him. I will be able to go home.

"If you kill me, my men will kill Lucy," Julian says.

How the hell does he know about Lucy? No one knows. Not even my best friends know.

But Julian's snicker says it all—I won't be killing Julian, at least not until I can ensure Lucy is safe.

3

—————

SIREN

I TURN to follow Zeke out of the room, when I hear Julian's voice. "We have a deal. Don't defy me again, Aria."

His words chill me for so many reasons. For seven years, I've regretted my vow to Julian, but right now, I don't. Because that vow led me here. And that vow kept me alive. And it led me to Zeke. And now I can save him.

I run out of the room without another word. I chase Zeke outside and go to jump into his truck. But when I reach for the handle, the door is locked. He doesn't look at me, but I swear I see a hint of a snicker at the corner of his lip. He knows what he's doing—shutting me out.

It's a short jog to his house, and the weather is abnormally cold, but I'm not worried about the walk. I fear that I'm permanently shut out. That Zeke won't let me in again. That he's locked me out forever.

I start walking down the street toward his house, when the skies open up, and a loud thunder rolls through. Then raindrops start pouring down, and my easy walk turns into an uncomfortable slog. It's like the weather itself is against me now, in addition to Zeke.

Fuck you, rain! All I've ever done is the right, unselfish thing, and it's turned the entire world against me. Everyone hates me—my husband, Zeke, even Julian is pissed. But the only person I care about liking me is Zeke. I need him to like me enough to at least listen to me.

I reach the doorstep of Zeke's house completely soaked, not exactly the look I was going for to tell Zeke the truth. Or at least enough of the truth to set him free.

I knock on the door loudly as the wind picks up and the rain starts blowing sideways. It's the tropics, but when it decides to rain like this, it can turn cold quickly. I shiver, crossing my arms over my body and rubbing my hands up and down my arms, trying to stay warm.

I listen for Zeke's footsteps to come open the door, but I don't hear him move. He can't hide from me; his truck is parked in the drive.

I pound on the door, loud enough that there is no denying he can hear me, even over the howl of the wind trying to knock me into the door. But still, Zeke doesn't answer.

I may have hardly cracked the surface when it comes to understanding Zeke, but I know that if it were up to Zeke, he and I would never speak again.

"Open up! I know you are inside, Zeke."

I pound again.

No answer.

"I'll break the door down!" I yell.

I hear footsteps this time, and I smile—*finally*. I hear the clink of the lock as Zeke turns it. And then nothing.

He doesn't open the door. This is as far as he'll go, unlocking the door so he doesn't have to deal with the hassle of replacing a broken door.

I grab the doorknob and push my way inside.

Zeke is no longer standing on the other side of the door. He isn't waiting for me or greeting me. He's going to ignore me.

I shiver as I step inside, my wet shoes leaving water tracks wherever I walk, and my soaked hair is dripping down my face. I should go try and find some clothes to change into—something to warm myself up, so I don't get pneumonia. But I need to see Zeke first.

It's selfish to see Zeke right now when he's so hurt. I should have told him the truth about Hugo. He shouldn't have found out that way. But there is so much Zeke doesn't know. So much he can never know.

I thought if Zeke thought the worst of me, I could save him easier. But it turns out I can't stand for Zeke to truly hate me, to shut me out, and never protect me even if it's for the best. *I need him to like me, just not save me.*

I march through the house—the kitchen, the bedroom, the sitting room. Zeke isn't in any of the rooms.

What?

Did he immediately run out of the house in this storm to avoid talking to me?

I turn to head to the front of the house to check if his truck is still here, when I spot his dark hair outside.

He's leaning against the side of the house, with a whiskey in his hand, as he stares out at the rain. He's standing close enough to the house that the rain can't touch him. But it still seems like a stupid move when a crack of lighting roars overhead.

I open the door. "Zeke!"

He doesn't turn. Or speak. Or even blink.

Zeke ignores me completely.

I became dead to him as soon as he found out I was married. Which is a fair way for Zeke to respond. But only because he doesn't know the truth. He doesn't know that my marriage isn't a marriage at all. It never was. Not really. I'm trapped into staying, and I can't do anything to get out of the marriage.

I step out next to Zeke, the rain pouring down on half of my body.

"Zeke!" I try again.

He sips his whiskey, deaf to my words.

Maybe it's for the best. I can get my side of the story out without him interrupting. He can pretend he can't hear me all he wants, but try as he might, he won't be able to resist listening.

"I didn't run to Hugo's side because I was worried. I ran to Hugo's side because I needed to know if he was alive or dead. I needed to know—"

"Enough," Zeke says, with one word sinking all of his indignation into me.

I close my eyes, forcing my pain inside. A tear escapes anyway. The rain hitting my face quickly washes it away, hiding my agony at being so close to him, at finally allowing myself to feel my love for Zeke, while accepting his hate.

"You deserve the truth," I say, opening my eyes and discerning the anger on Zeke's face. His eyes are red with passion, his body stiff with rage.

"I deserve more than the truth, but I'm not going to get it from you."

"Let me try," I say firmly. He needs to know the truth. At least part of it. Enough so that his hate softens. It will never go away, I hurt him too much, but maybe he can see that the brief times we spent together were real. The feelings we sparked—real. All of it was real. And I wouldn't take a second of it back.

"No. Go back to your husband," Zeke says, finishing his drink.

I take a deep breath, knowing that he won't listen. That my time is running out.

"I'm sorry," I say, meaning my words more than any others I've spoken to him. If I could pour everything I'm feeling into those two words, we would be standing here all day. But I try in the single moment Zeke gives me.

Zeke turns sideways until he is facing me, half of his body is now getting pounded with rain, same as me.

"What exactly are you sorry for, Siren? Sorry for lying? For cheating on your husband? For betraying me again?" Zeke's voice doesn't need the entire day to express his feelings. It's clear he's only feeling one thing—anger.

"For all of it," I answer, not backing down even though it looks like he's about to hit me. Zeke may be angry, but he'd never hit me. He can pretend he's a vicious man with everyone but me.

Zeke takes another step toward me, blocking some of the rain from my face. I want him to kiss me. To put his hands on me. To touch me. Give me any amount of hope that we will get one more night together if we can't have forever.

He doesn't touch me; his eyes command me—tell me exactly what he wants me to do.

And for once, I do as he commands. I step aside and watch him walk inside. Leaving me for the second time in twenty-four hours without a chance to explain my truth.

I reach out to grab the door, to prevent him from locking me out, but I miss. Instead, our fingers brush. Zeke freezes at our electric touch. I've never felt such a spark with a man before. I thought for sure it would be gone. It would have been easier to let Zeke go if it was. And I know Zeke would have preferred it that way.

The spark isn't gone. In fact, I feel it deeper into my soul than I've ever felt it before. Zeke feels it too. It's why he's frozen in place. We can fight our love for each other all we want, but we can't fight our attraction, our physical connection. It won't go away. Not now. *Not ever.*

Zeke finally snaps out of it, he walks into the house, leaving me standing in the rain. It's what I deserve in his eyes, and what I wanted—for him to shut me out. But it's the most painful thing I can imagine. I'd rather be dead than live in a world where Zeke hates me, and yet, that's exactly the world I created.

4

ZEKE

Two women keep floating around in my head. Both of them kept me up all night, and not for good reasons. I didn't get to kiss or fuck either of them.

Lucy Greene.

Jesus, I haven't thought that name in years. I never thought I'd think that name again. I thought Lucy was out of my life forever. No one knows about our past. At least, that was what I thought until Julian mentioned her name.

How in the hell does he know about Lucy?

She was my ultimate secret.

The one piece of my life that wasn't tainted with darkness.

But now that Julian knows about her, I have to act. I have to go back to the one light spot in my life. The one woman who I thought would never enter my new life. None of my friends or family knew about her. So I have no idea how Julian knows about her, but I will fight to the death to keep Lucy safe.

Lucy is a true angel. She's innocent. Sweet, kind, a school

teacher. She volunteered at animal shelters. She was the perfect woman if one was ever to exist.

I should have spent my entire night coming up with a plan to keep her safe. A way to safely contact her. A plan to find out how Julian found her. Because if he found her, anyone could.

That's what I was doing outside as I looked out at the storm. But then Siren walked outside and consumed my thoughts.

Siren looked hot as sin standing outside in the rain, her clothes clinging to her body, revealing every curve. And then she shivered, and I got the urge to wrap my arms around her. To carry her inside, rip her wet clothes from her body, and warm her up.

But then I remembered—*she's not mine*. She never was. She may not be Hugo's either. But she certainly isn't mine.

The outrage came back, keeping me from touching her. Followed by the resentment, the double-cross, and finally the need to fuck her harder than I ever have before, until I make her mine only to tell her that I don't want her.

All I let her see was the anger.

I did everything right. I ignored her. Yelled at her. Refused to let her tell her side of the story. If she isn't talking and I'm not looking at her, then her lies can't hurt me.

I did everything right and yet...*I made one mistake*. I let our hands touch. It wasn't so much a mistake as an accident. I thought I could control my feelings. I thought any attraction I felt for her left my body the second she said she was married. I don't fuck married women, no matter their circumstances. I don't do cheaters, and backstabbers, and liars.

But what the fuck was with that touch?

How can one touch knock all sense from my head?

I've never felt anything like it. It's like her body is calling to me, and when we touch, it's the only way my body can operate at full power. Without her, I feel like I'm slowly being drained of all my energy, and the second our fingers brushed together, I came alive.

She's just messing with my head again. She doesn't care about me, and I don't care about her. *So what if we have physical attraction?* I can find that again with any girl. It's just been too long since I've been with another woman. I can find the spark again.

I spent the night shutting Siren out of my room. I didn't speak to her. And I didn't let her into my room. But it didn't stop her from speaking.

I tried not to listen, really I did.

But she said everything I was desperate to hear—*I don't love Hugo. I'm not sure I ever did.*

Eventually, I threw a pillow over my head to drown her out. And at some point in the night, she gave up, because when I woke up, Siren was gone.

I may have spent too much time last night thinking about Siren. But this morning, it's clear what my next step is.

I grab my keys, jump in my truck, and head back to the hospital. I know Julian and Siren are my enemies. But I need to know if I have one ally. Julian was the one who put Hugo in the hospital. Siren cheated on him. Maybe Hugo's on my side. Although, when he finds out I'm the one who's been sleeping with his wife, that may change.

Still, I need information, and Hugo might be my best bet to get it. He may be the only one who hates Julian more than I do.

I park in the parking lot and walk inside. I smile at the receptionist who remembers me from the other night and tells me that Hugo has been moved to a regular room.

The hospital is small, and there are only two main hallways, which makes it easy to find Hugo's room.

My temper flares when I see who is occupying his room —*Siren.*

Their conversation stops, and both of their heads snap to me as I step in. I walk in like I own the place. My plan is to ignore Siren and show Hugo just how powerful I am and that he shouldn't mess with me, at least until I figure out if he's on my side or not.

But when I see Siren's hand resting on Hugo's leg, I can't help myself. "You sure do spend a lot of time here for a woman who claims she doesn't love her husband."

Siren rolls her eyes like my jab didn't hurt her, but I know her well enough now—*it does.*

The reaction I care more about is Hugo's. He doesn't seem surprised at all to learn that his supposed wife doesn't love him. He just eats his Jello with a small smile.

Hugo looks horrible. There are bruises and cuts everywhere. Tubes connect into his arm and chest. A cast wraps around his right leg.

But the way he's moving happily and eating without difficulty feels off. I've had full body injuries like him before, and I could barely breathe, let alone eat twenty-four hours after it happened. *How can he move so easily? Even with pain medication?*

And this hospital looks like it's barely standing upright, let alone able to handle his extensive injuries. That was why Siren took me to Julian to get me medical help. This hospital can't handle severe injuries. Something isn't right.

I look from Hugo to Siren. She's an expert at figuring out liars and deceit. Yet, if she realizes something is off, she doesn't let on. *Unless she's in on the deceit?*

Fuck, I can't trust anything when it comes to Siren. This was a mistake; I shouldn't be here. I can't trust Hugo anymore than I can trust Siren.

"And you are?" Hugo asks.

"The man who slept with your wife," I answer. Not really the best way to get this man on my side, but I want everything out in the open. And I want to hurt Siren as much as I can.

Siren glares at me. "This is Zeke Kane. He owes a debt to Julian."

Hugo stops eating his Jello as he looks from Siren to me. And I know immediately that he wants her. He may not love her. And I may not understand what happened in their marriage, but the desire is there. Siren's eyes don't look at Hugo, though. They sink into me, straight to my heart. Like she knows why I'm here, and she thinks I'm stupid to trust Hugo. Her eyes tell me not to trust Hugo. Which gives me even more reason to trust him.

Hugo wants Siren, but what does Siren want? Who does she love? If she loves Hugo, it makes me want to hurt him just to hurt her. And if she loves me...*she doesn't, so it doesn't matter.*

My guess is she loves no one. She's a selfish minx incapable of love.

I turn my attention back to Hugo. It doesn't matter who Siren loves or even who Hugo loves. It matters who Hugo is loyal to.

"I'm Zeke, and I'm looking for an ally. Are you that man, Hugo? Do you hate Julian Reed?"

Hugo throws back the rest of the Jello into his mouth like he's doing a shot, then swallows with a big smile.

"No one hates Julian Reed more than I do," Hugo answers.

I grin. "I do."

5

———

SIREN

I LOOK BACK and forth between the two men. One is my asshole of a husband. The other—a man I wish was my husband.

These men should hate each other's guts. Hugo is my technical husband, who I never told Zeke about. Zeke feels betrayed because I'm married, even if it's only on paper.

And even though Hugo has slept with countless women since we've been married, he should hate that Zeke has been the one warming my bed.

Instead, these two men just made an arrangement. They became allies with a couple of words and a handshake.

What. The. Hell.

This can't be happening. I must be dreaming. I must have lost my mind. I'm sleep deprived from sitting outside Zeke's bedroom door all night, wishing I didn't have to be the devil in disguise for just once. But I don't think I could dream up an entire conversation. *Could I?*

Zeke nods at Hugo. "Rest up and get better. I'll check up on you when your wife isn't here, and we can talk gameplan."

It's happening. Zeke is talking about making a gameplan to take out Julian.

"I look forward to it," Hugo answers.

No, no, no! These two men are supposed to be enemies. Hate, not love each other.

Zeke starts walking out the door as I'm still gaping in shock. That was the last thing I expected to have to worry about.

Hugo raises his eyebrow at me, just as shocked by the turn of events as I am. But unlike me, Hugo just grabs another Jello off his tray and goes back to eating while he flips the TV back on to some baseball game.

Ugh.

I'll deal with Hugo later. He's not going anywhere. Although, he's surprisingly chipper today for someone who was just hit by a car.

Instead, I run after Zeke.

"Zeke," I snap, when I reach the hallway and see him about to round the corner. I don't expect him to stop, to give me any time to talk. *He didn't last night, why should he today?*

Maybe it's the desperation in my voice. Maybe it's the heartbreak he wants to stick around and witness. Maybe he wants to rub his new alliance in my face. Maybe he's just tired of ignoring me and wants to have it out.

Whatever the reason, he stops.

I jog down the hallway to where he's standing in the hallway of the small hospital. I don't want to have this conversation here in public, but I doubt Zeke will follow me somewhere more private.

"What are you doing?" I ask as I stand a foot away from him. So close, yet so far. What I really want to do is throw my arms around him and kiss him. Remind him that he likes me if not loves me.

He puts his hands in the pocket of his jeans as he tilts his head with a smile. He hasn't shaved, and the scruff on his face makes me drool. And he wore his hair down, just how I like it—the bastard. He knows exactly what he's doing—driving me insane with need. He's trying to play me like he thinks I played him. The only difference is, I wasn't playing him for my own enjoyment. I was playing him to protect him.

"Why would I tell you anything, Siren?"

"Don't work with Hugo."

"Hugo is your husband. I would think you would want me to work with him."

"You shouldn't trust Hugo. He only looks out for himself. He's only interested in money."

"I trust him more than I trust you."

I close my eyes at the impact of his words. He has no reason to trust me. *None*. But it still hurts. Like a knife to the chest.

I miss the old Zeke. The Zeke who would protect me with his life. The Zeke who would bring me coffee and flowers for no reason. The Zeke who was a romantic deep down. This Zeke is cold and calculated. This Zeke is closed up.

"Don't, Zeke. Don't trust Hugo. If you want to work with him, fine. But don't let your guard down with him." I can't look at Zeke. Seeing him hurts. Being near him and not touching him hurts. Seeing how pissed he is at me hurts. Because all I want to do is explain. If I could show him my heart, I would. Because my heart holds the truth.

Zeke's fingers go under my chin, tilting up so that I look at him. He looks into my eyes, like he can tell all of my secrets. I wish he could. Then he would know the truth.

His words still hang in the air—I trust him more than I trust you.

Zeke has no idea who Hugo is. He has no idea that on a scale of an angel to devil, Hugo falls second only to the devil himself. I may have once thought of him as an innocent, but now I know that he and Julian are more alike than different. The main difference is that Julian tells you exactly who he is, while Hugo hides his monster better beneath layers of charm and pretty blue eyes.

"You trust Hugo more than this," I say, and then I do something wonderfully stupid.

I grab Zeke's T-shirt and close the gap. He opens his mouth to speak, but it's too late. Our lips have collided in one hungry kiss—his eyes hood and then close. And then I let my eyes fall closed.

He doesn't fight the kiss like I expect, but I keep my grip on his shirt just in case. Zeke may not let me explain with my words, but maybe I can explain with my tongue.

The kiss is open-mouthed. It's the kind of messy kiss that involves teeth clashing and heads tilting the wrong way to make the most of the kiss. It's sloppy; our tongues battle each other in a frenzy.

But the kiss still does things to my heart. It makes it beat harder. It gives me hope. It sets me on fire.

And from the erection poking me in the stomach, I know that it does things to Zeke too.

Someone moans. *Me? Him? Both?*

And then his hands start greedily exploring my body. Over my ass, then under my shirt.

He wants me. He can hate me all he wants, but his hate won't stop him from fucking me.

I should want him to like me before I let him fuck me

again, but I need this. And sometimes, fucking can lead to more truths than words can.

A throat clears.

"If you are going to continue on like this, I suggest the hotel up the street."

We both stop, turning our heads to face the surly nurse who is grimacing at us. My leg has somehow wrapped itself around Zeke's hip. His hand is on my ass. My hand still grips his shirt. And I know my hair is completely disheveled.

The nurse walks away, satisfied that we will stop making out in the hallway of the hospital like two unruly teenagers.

Slowly, Zeke lowers my leg, and he removes his hand from my ass. I loosen my grip on his shirt and run my hand through my hair. And then we separate.

I have no words, and yet, I have so much to say. Zeke doesn't give me the time to speak, though.

He clears his throat, and I think for a moment he's going to speak, but it seems he's just clearing his head of his impure thoughts as much as he's readying his throat to speak.

And then he's walking away, leaving me standing in the hallway with no answers.

"Zeke!" I shout again.

He doesn't turn this time.

"Promise me you won't trust Hugo," I yell after him.

He pauses for the briefest of seconds and then continues walking out of the hospital. Zeke doesn't make me any promises.

I stand in the hallway, torn between running after him and returning to Hugo. Right now, the best way to protect Zeke is to keep him away from this idiotic deal. And if Zeke won't listen to me, I know a man who has no choice but to listen to me as he's stuck in a hospital bed.

I storm back to Hugo's room. The look I give him is full of anger and rage. My eyes shoot into him like bladed knives.

Hugo chuckles. "Really? You going to give me that look when you've probably just fucked the guy while still married to me?"

I march over to his bed and yank the remote from his hand before turning off the TV.

Hugo huffs.

"You are not going to work with Zeke, under any circumstances. You are not allies. You are not friends. You are nothing to each other. Understand?"

Hugo smiles. "You don't get to tell me who I can and can't work with."

"Yes, I can."

"No, you can't. We're married; you aren't my boss. You have nothing on me. You're the reason I'm in this hospital bed, in fact. If anything, *you owe me*, not the other way around."

I cross my arms, glaring at him and wishing that car accident had killed him. It might have been on my conscious that Julian killed him because of me, but I'd rather have that than put Zeke at risk.

"You will stay away from Zeke," I say.

"And what will you do for me?" Hugo's smile cuts deep into me. It's not a happy smile; it's a smile that says I own you.

I may not be a slave, but it doesn't stop me from being owned. Three men own me, all in different ways.

Julian owns my actions and loyalty.

Hugo owns my name and past.

And Zeke owns my heart.

Someday, I won't be owned anymore. Someday, I will claim everything back. Everything except my heart.

Today isn't that day, though. Today, I have to save the man I love—a man who, even after one betrayal, continued to protect me—only giving me up after I betrayed him twice, both in unforgivable ways.

"How much?" I ask.

Hugo's smile falters. "You really think my loyalty can be bought?"

"I know it can. All you care about is money."

He shakes his head. "Oh, Aria, my sweet. You really don't know me at all."

"One million, all you have to do is avoid Zeke, stay the hell away from him. It will be the easiest money you've ever earned."

"No."

"Two million."

"No."

"Five million."

"And who exactly will you be stealing this money from, Aria?" He laughs. "You don't have that kind of pocket change."

I glare. "You don't know me that well."

He leans forward. "I do know you that well. And we're married. So if you have five million stashed somewhere, half of it is mine."

I frown. Money apparently isn't the way to go with him.

"What do you want, then?"

His eyes run up and down my body in a slow, seductive way, telling me exactly what he wants—me, on my knees, sucking his cock before I spread my legs for him.

"Not going to happen." I flip my hair. Although, I would.

I'd fuck him if it meant saving Zeke. Surely, I can find a better way to convince Hugo just to stay the hell away from him.

I sit down on the edge of his hospital bed, turning up my charm as I take his hand in mine. I rub my thumb across the back of his hand in a slow, teasing way I used to when we were teens. "What else do you want, Hugo?"

"You can play your games on me all you want, Aria, it won't work. I know all your tricks." He grabs my hand with his other hand, forcing me to stop.

I sigh.

"What do you want, Hugo? I know you don't want to work with Zeke. What will it take to get you to stay away?"

He grins, and I know exactly what he's going to say before he says it. And it's the one thing I'm desperate for yet can't have because of what it will mean.

"I want a divorce, Aria."

I suck in a breath. *So do I, but the consequences of getting a divorce are too great.*

I stand up, done with this conversation. My hands falling from his as I walk to the door. I tried with Zeke. I tried with Hugo. But in the end, I lost my fight with both. I have to find a different way to keep them from working with each other.

"Tell me when you're ready for that divorce," Hugo says as I walk out the door.

I stiffen, not letting him get to me. As I round the corner, I spot something on my hand and stop. There's a red substance on my fingers, similar in color to blood. But it's not.

Dammit, Hugo.

And suddenly, I know exactly why Hugo wants to work with Zeke. Not because he hates Julian, but because Julian is paying him to be in that hospital bed. And none of it is real. He's not really hurt. It was all a lie. He never got hit by a car. I don't know when Hugo went from being Julian's enemy to his ally, but I'm going to figure it out. And my vow to Julian to protect Hugo's life just went out the window in my book.

6

—————

ZEKE

That motherfucking kiss.

Why did she have to go and do that?

Or did I initiate the kiss?

I can't remember. It just happened. Like neither of us had any control over whether we would kiss or not. It was inevitable.

It should have felt like poison to my lips. The kiss should have tasted bitter.

But of course, what my mind thinks and what my body feels is constantly at odds. I can never get my body to feel what my mind tells it to.

Fuck!

I throw my whiskey glass across the room and watch it shatter against the far wall of my kitchen, its contents rolling down a cabinet. It's much too early to be drinking anyway. But the outburst does nothing to tamper my pent up frustration.

When did everything in my life get so fucking complicated?

I used to have an easy life. I worked for my best friend. I was the muscle of the group that got things done. Not the man tied up in drama, women, and complications. But that's my life right now.

I almost want to march over to Julian's and demand he gives me another task just so I have something physical to do. I'd love to kill a man with my bare hands right now.

A soft rattling at my front door stops those thoughts. Because I know exactly who is standing behind that door —Siren.

And instantly, all my thoughts shift to her. I just can't make sense of my feelings. You know that game—fuck, marry, kill? You are supposed to choose one for each person in your life. Who you'd fuck, who you'd marry, and who you'd kill. With Siren, I don't want to choose just one. I want to do all three.

Dammit, why'd I have to go and throw my drink? I'm going to need it to get through this conversation. I need to use it as armor to keep her away from me, so I don't do something stupider than that kiss.

I open the door and find Siren standing on my porch. I glance behind her and spot a red corvette behind her. *Where'd the car come from?* Usually, she takes a cab if I don't drive her. Or that beat-up thing I've seen her drive in the past.

It's Hugo's.

"You can't trust Hugo," Siren says, pushing past me to come inside without waiting to be invited.

I roll my eyes. "Yes, please come in. I don't hate you or anything. You haven't betrayed my trust every chance you get. Shouldn't you be telling me not to trust *you*?"

She ignores me. *Probably smart.*

She throws off her leather jacket, revealing her toned arms and giving me a better view of her tits beneath her thin white shirt.

She notices where my eyes have landed.

"Zeke, this is important," she huffs, putting her hands on her hips, which only makes her boobs look bigger.

I let my eyes drift up lazily. "You have five minutes to talk, and then I want you out of my house forever." I don't add that I want her out of my life as well. But not before I fuck her, then marry her, then kill her.

"Hugo is working with Julian. The car accident wasn't real. He faked it," Siren says.

I walk over to my bar. *Yep, this conversation is definitely going to require a drink.* At least a glass in my hand will keep me sane or give me something to throw at her when she pisses me off.

"Zeke, are you listening? Did you hear what I said? You can't work with Hugo because he's working with Julian."

I pour the scotch three fingers high. *Yep, I'm going to need every drop.*

"Zeke!" Siren grabs my arm, and I spill a couple of drops of the scotch.

"Why the fuck did you do that?"

"Listen to me! You can't work with Hugo. Not because you think it will somehow get under my skin to be working with my ex."

I lift the glass to my lips. "You mean current husband."

She rolls her eyes. "Hugo is an ex, trust me."

"I don't."

She sighs. "You can't work with Hugo because he's working with Julian. Together they faked the accident. Why, I don't know, but I'm guessing to try and manipulate us both."

I take a sip. "Are you finished?"

"That's all you have to say?" She crosses her arms and pouts her adorable lips in the way that says she's not going to let this conversation end until I agree with her. And I do agree with her, but I hate letting her win. I prefer to watch her squirm like she is now. But I said only five minutes, and I'm sure our time is about up.

"I know," I say just as she opens her mouth to spill more info that will convince me of Hugo's loyalty.

"Wait... you know?"

"Yes."

"How?"

"Because it doesn't take Sherlock Holmes to figure out that Hugo wasn't in a major car accident. I've been through enough accidents to know that you don't just sit up in bed and eat Jello the next day. And that hospital doesn't have the capabilities to save a man from major injuries anyway. It's why you took me to Julian to save my life." *Dammit, I forgot she saved my life.* Although after everything that's happened since, I'm not sure if it was a blessing or a curse.

She leans against the counter, her head falling back. "How'd I miss all of that?"

I run my hand through my hair because I know exactly how you miss all the obvious signs that someone is lying to you. "Because you fell for him. You loved him. Even if you don't currently. People become blinded by love."

Our eyes meet, and the unspoken past slides between us —*love.* Neither of us ever said it. I was close to feeling it. The closest I've ever been with a woman. But I never said it. And now, I never will.

It wasn't love. It was attraction, lust, loneliness. I saw a pretty woman who was smart and a fighter, and I fell. That's all; it wasn't love—just me falling out of my orbit.

"So, you won't work with Hugo?"

I take a drink, hoping to avoid this conversation. Because there is no reasonable explanation I can give her as to why I need to work with Hugo. Even knowing the truth, without telling her about Lucy. And enough people already know about her. I can't risk her life by telling Siren about her as well. It's a miracle she didn't hear Julian whisper into my ear. Although, there's a good chance he will eventually tell Siren about Lucy. I won't be the one to be disloyal to Lucy, though.

"Zeke?" Siren's voice is full of hesitation, because she can read me too well. She knows that I'm avoiding.

"How can you still work with him when he isn't on your side? Why?"

Because I need to know everything they know about Lucy. I need someone that I may be able to flip. Someone who is vulnerable. Someone I can use as leverage. And Hugo Martinez seems like the perfect man.

Julian wants me to fall for his tricks. So I'll let him think I fell.

I look at Siren with a raised eyebrow. "I've worked with plenty of people who aren't on my side."

Her face falls when she realizes I mean her.

And then she walks over to my bar and grabs the scotch bottle. She takes a swig straight from the bottle as if she needs the courage to say what she needs to say next.

"We haven't had sex," she says.

My head snaps to her. Whatever I expected her to say that wasn't it. I expected her to try and convince me to not work with Hugo. Not tell me something honest about herself.

"Well, that's not true entirely. Hugo and I haven't had sex since we were married."

My mouth falls open into a huge gape. I don't know what to say to that. She wants it to change things. But I won't let it. She lied to me about being married. No, she never said she was married, but she manipulated me into thinking she wasn't married, which is somehow worse.

Then she used me to cheat on her husband. I don't care how horrible he is. If he's that bad, then divorce his ass. Or at least tell me the truth, so I can decide if I want to participate in her infidelity. So I can at least protect my heart from falling for a married woman.

"Is that supposed to make it better that you cheated on him with me?" I ask.

She takes another sip of the scotch and then puts the bottle back before hopping up on my counter with her hands in her lap. She looks so young sitting there like that. Not like that strong independent traitor of a woman I know she is.

"No, it's just the truth. You want the truth? I'll tell you."

I'm not sure I want the truth, not anymore. Not from her. But apparently, I do because I don't tell her any of that. And I listen like I might fall off a cliff if I don't catch every syllable she speaks.

"We fucked one night in the backseat of my car."

"The same one you rescued me in?"

She nods.

Shit, now I know I really hate that car.

"Hugo was my first. It wasn't perfect. It wasn't magical. It was messy and painful and uncomfortable. But that was my life."

God, I really don't want to hear about how another guy took her virginity. But I don't stop her from talking.

"But I knew afterward that he was the man for me. I didn't want perfect. I didn't want romance. I wanted real. And Hugo was as real as it got. He taught me self-defense. He taught me how to play guitar. Encourage me to write songs, to sing to get through the pain of my childhood instead of turning to drugs. He saved my life. He brought me back to life."

Siren can play guitar? God, I would do anything to hear it. And she writes her own songs. I'm desperate to hear just one of them. What would she write about me?

"So when I found out the truth—that the reason Hugo didn't want me doing drugs was because he was already addicted. That he sold drugs to make enough money to buy them. That he was in huge debt and was going to be killed if he couldn't pay it back. I did everything to save him."

How does this story make me wish that I was Hugo? She already saved your ass as well. Hugo isn't special. Tell me more...

"I tried to steal something valuable enough from Julian to pay off Hugo's debt. But Julian caught me. I thought I was going to die, but he offered me a trade. He would pay off Hugo's debt, if I worked for him for ten years. I agreed. I would have done anything."

Anything.

"So I went back to Hugo. We got married. And then I went to Julian to work. I thought Hugo would wait for me. I thought we'd get our happily ever after eventually. We were young, after all. Ten years was nothing. And we could still see each other whenever Julian didn't demand work from me. But the first chance I had to go home, I caught Hugo with another woman in our bed. A woman he'd been fucking our entire relationship."

I can feel her heart breaking. I want to run to her. I want to protect her. Comfort her. But I can't. I can't show her that I care.

"Do you have any idea the pain I felt at having a man I loved betray me like that? I gave up ten years of my life to save him? And he was cheating on me the whole time."

"I have an idea," I say.

And then I see a tear roll down her cheek, and I break. I can't just watch her cry without doing something.

Slowly, I walk over to her. She leans away, thinking I'm going to make fun of her pain.

Maybe a stronger man would have. But if there is one thing I understand better than most, it's pain and heartbreak. And I don't wish that kind of pain on my worst enemy. I'd rather be shot than deal with a broken heart.

Carefully, I reach my thumb up to her cheek and brush away the tear. Careful, not to do more than just touch the tear. *Don't let any feelings in. Don't give her the wrong idea.*

"You've never fucked him since you got married?"

"No."

"Have you fucked other men?"

She nods. "I wanted to hurt him for what he did to me. So for a while there, I fucked every man I could find just to hurt him."

She means she fucked any man she could to numb her own pain. I understand; I feel the same way.

"In some states, you wouldn't be considered married, since you never consummated the marriage," I say.

She smiles, weakly. "Do you consider me married? Because I don't. It's only real on paper."

I lean forward and smell her hair. *Fuck.*

"You aren't getting out of your betrayal on a technicality."

"I'm not trying to," she breathes back. "I just want to know what you think. Am I married or not?"

I take a step back. *Don't fall for it. Don't fall under her spell. It could all be a lie.*

"Why are you still married to him? Why didn't you divorce his ass as soon as you found that whore in bed with him?"

She smiles when I call the woman a whore. "I can't."

Julian said as much. "Does it have something to do with a prenup?"

"Yes."

"Why sign something if you knew it would trap you in a marriage forever?"

"Because I thought it was forever. I loved him. It didn't matter what the prenup said."

"What did it say?"

She shakes her head. Apparently, it's the one truth I won't be getting. "It says that I will be married to Hugo Martinez until one of us dies."

I sigh. One step forward in the truth with her and two steps back.

"Do you still love him?"

"No, seeing him in that hospital bed confirmed it. When I went to the hospital, I wasn't sure what I felt. My feelings were complicated when it comes to Hugo."

I nod. *My feelings are complicated when it comes to you.*

"Divorce him," I say.

Her eyes flutter, shocked.

"Divorce him. Whatever you have to pay him. Whatever you have to give up, it's worth it to be rid of him."

She doesn't answer back, but I have a feeling she will never divorce him. Which means I have to let her the fuck go.

"Can I kill him since you obviously won't divorce him?"

She sucks in a breath but then shakes her head no.

"Why not? You hate him. He's ruined your life. Most women who were cheated like that would want him dead or at least tortured for what he did."

She looks off into the distance past me. "I loved Hugo once. Really loved him. And I think even though he was cheating on me, that for one magical moment, he loved me too. And as much as I want to hurt him for hurting me, for ruining my life, I can't betray those people we once were. I can't denounce that love. Because it was real. And it was special. It was everything. And if I ever have hope of feeling that again, I have to believe in love. That love exists and that it should never be crossed. Even when both people fall out of love. Even when two people fall into hate."

Like us.

But we never fell in love. We came close. But it never happened. She stopped it from happening.

Siren wipes her eyes and then rolls her shoulders. This conversation is over.

"I think my five minutes are up." She jumps down from the counter. "Do what you need to do when it comes to Hugo. But just know that he can manipulate people just like I can. And unlike me, he has no problem lying with his words. So make sure you are the one doing the betraying this time."

She starts walking toward my front door. Leaving me for the first time on her own accord.

And for once, a small part of me doesn't want her to go.

"Siren," I say.

She stops. "Yes?"

"Ask me again."

She narrows her eyes, trying to understand what I want her to repeat. A moment passes, then another.

"Do you consider my marriage to Hugo real?"

"No."

She smiles lightly and then walks out the door. And I know I've fucked up because I just sparked a hope that will never happen. Siren will never be mine, and I'll never fall for her again. She may not be in a real marriage, but she's lied and betrayed me enough that I can never trust her again. I shouldn't give her hope. I shouldn't give myself hope. I should be cold and calculated with her.

But maybe I need to think that in a different universe, we would have a chance. One in which we didn't have other people to be loyal to. One in which we always told each other the truth and always chose the other person over everyone else.

I need hope that in some other universe, we are living together happily ever after. Because in this world, all we are ever going to do is destroy each other.

7
———

SIREN

ZEKE GAVE ME HOPE, and somehow that is worse than making sure he ended things between us for good. Because now I have hope. Now my heart flutters in my chest, pretending that I'm about to become Mrs. Zeke Kane, instead of being stuck with a name I hate.

No, I'm not Aria Martinez married to the asshole Hugo Martinez. Zeke said so himself—our marriage isn't real.

But I'm not Siren Kane either.

I'm Aria Torres.

I'm an expert manipulator, man-hater, and slayer of men.

Even after my last three years are up with Julian, this is who I will always be. I don't even know how to hold down a normal job anymore. I've been doing this for Julian for so long. And some part of me likes it. I like making men pay for their crimes. I like traveling. I like the adventure. The control. The power.

I like it all.

The only thing I don't like is having to answer to other men. Men like Julian Reed and Hugo Martinez.

48

But somehow I'm not sure I'd mind answering to Zeke Kane. Although, I'd argue back and want him to listen to me as much as I listen to him.

Fuck hope.

I don't get to have hope.

This is my life. And my goal hasn't changed. I need to get Zeke free of this world and back into his. Zeke thinks Hugo can help him do that, but he's wrong.

I've played all the cards I have when it comes to Zeke. But I have one card left to play with Hugo. And I'm going to play it.

I drive recklessly fast back to the hospital, where Hugo is lying with a fake injury.

And as I make the last turn, I spot a familiar-looking truck driving just as recklessly behind me.

Really Zeke? You say you want me out of your life, yet you won't leave me alone for five minutes when I want to do something by myself.

That's okay. He can watch the show and see how weak Hugo is. Zeke can see how he doesn't really want him on his side.

I park my Corvette illegally in a no parking zone. I don't care if it gets towed. It's Hugo's car anyway. I prefer beat-up, older cars. Cars with plenty of muscle, heart, and grit. Just like I like my men.

I strut inside. If this was a bar, I'd be turning heads. I nod at the woman behind the nurses' station, but I'm not stopping. I'm pretty sure it's still visiting hours, but even if it isn't, I'm not letting that stop me.

I throw the door open to Hugo's room; his eyes pop away from the stupid TV he's been watching all day.

Carefully, I close the door behind me, wishing the door had a lock, but it won't take long to do what I need to do.

"You fucking, lying bastard," I say.

Hugo cocks his head to the side as he flicks off the television. "And why would you say that?"

"Because it's fucking true."

I march over to his bed with more fury in my eyes than when I caught him fucking another woman in the bed I bought for him.

And I'm rewarded with him recoiling into his bed like the slime that he is. I love this power that I have in this moment. And I almost don't want to do the next step because once you use your power, it starts fleeting. You can never be as powerful as you are when you make the threat and display. When you enact the threat, your power starts slipping until you earn it again.

I grab Hugo's hospital gown and jerk him out of bed. He stands immediately, his hand holding onto mine.

"Oh, look at that. He can stand," I say, with vengeance in my eyes.

Hugo blinks rapidly. He wasn't expecting this.

Hugo may have taught me self-defense. He may have paid for classes for me to learn Krav Maga. But I've never used the skills I learned on him. Even when he cheated on me. *Today that changes.*

"Only because you're holding me up," he says.

I let go. "Still standing."

I take a step forward, forcing him to take a step back.

"Why are you working with Julian?"

He takes a step back.

"Why would you work for a man who trapped me in this life? I knew you couldn't keep your dick in your pants, but I never thought you were cruel."

"I'm not."

"Then, why?"

"I'm not working with Julian."

I take another step forward, and he takes his last step as the bed prevents him from walking further back.

"Don't lie. You weren't injured in a car accident. You faked it with makeup and the help of the nurses. Julian hired you."

"He thought it would be easier to control you if he controlled me. My choice was to work for him, or he'd actually have me run over by a car or shot. So forgive me for not wanting to get shot."

I laugh. "Forgive you? That's a poor choice of words. I'll never forgive you. And I would have taken the bullet every time rather than stab you in the back."

"No, you wouldn't have."

"I've worked for Julian for seven years because of you! I sure as hell would have taken a bullet for you. I loved you once. That's a mistake I'll never repeat."

I hear the door open, and I know we have an audience. I also know who it is. And it isn't some nurse coming to check on the commotion. I'm sure Julian paid off the nurses to ignore whatever happens in this room.

Julian may think he can manipulate Hugo in order to control me. But today is the last day that works. I will no longer protect Hugo. I'll no longer save him. From today on, he's on his own. We are enemies, not friends, not exes —enemies.

"This is for not taking a bullet for me when you should have," I say.

"Baby, you're not going to hurt me," Hugo says.

My eyes light up at his words. Hugo used to know me. He used to know what I'm capable of. But seven years of working for Julian has changed all of that.

Seven years has turned me bitter. Seven years is too long to go without getting revenge.

I grab his arm and slam him into the wall before he has a chance to react. Seven years has changed Hugo too. He's lived a cushy life with plenty of money since I set him free. Seven years of not having to look over his shoulder. His self-defense skills are weak.

He winces, his head rattling as it hits the wall.

"This is for me," I say, slamming his wrist into the wall until I hear little bones crack.

"And this is for Zeke," I say, head butting Hugo, breaking his nose.

I let go of Hugo and step back. He grabs his wrist, and his eyes water, barely containing his tears as he crumples to the floor in front of me.

"You are such a bitch!" He cries out, not bothering hiding his tears now as he cradles his wrist.

"And you're a cheating, lying cunt who now has the required injuries to warrant a hospital stay." I grin.

"Julian will hear about this."

"Good." I fold my arms across my chest. "He'll be happy to know my skills are still sharp. That I realized this was all a trick and handled the situation. Because Julian Reed doesn't give a shit about you, Hugo. He cares about me. I'm his prized possession. His armor. His secret weapon. And you are nothing but a game to him."

I crack my neck and flip my hair as I turn and look at Zeke, who is leaning against the wall with a smirk on his face. I wasn't sure how he was going to react. If he was going to be pissed that I'd outed Hugo's plan or happy.

But from the look of awe on his face, I think it's the latter.

"He's all yours," I say as I walk over to the chair in the

corner of the room and take a seat. I know Zeke came here on business of his own, but I'm not going to let him talk to Hugo alone.

Zeke shakes his head. "I'm never going to get over how you can bring a man to his knees." The way Zeke is looking at me with a wolfish expression makes me wonder what he means—how I brought Hugo to his knees in pain, or Zeke to his knees in lust.

8

———

ZEKE

Siren is the most kick-ass woman I've ever met. She doesn't need a man to take care of her. And she's been screwed over by enough men that even if she did need a man to protect her, she wouldn't take a man's help.

It gives me a little perspective on why she doesn't trust me and why she was willing to betray me. It doesn't make me forgive her or envision any future together. But it helps to understand.

To most men, Siren might be intimidating. She just broke her ex's wrist and nose. Sure, I'm bigger than her and could stop her if I really wanted to if she tried that shit on me. But she has the ability. And if she really wanted to break my wrist, she'd find a way.

Intimidating.

And so fucking sexy.

I've always been the romantic type. I enjoy taking care of women. But with Siren, I want to take care of her even more. Because I can see past the armor she wears, I can see that she's just as desperate to be taken care of as any other

54

woman, even if she is more than capable of taking care of herself.

She just broke her ex's wrist. But I don't think she did it for herself. She did it because he tried to mess with me. And that won't go unnoticed. *Why? Why did him possibly hurting me affect her more than when he fucked with her?*

I don't have time to analyze it right now. Siren just changed the plan. When I jumped in my car to come here, I debated continuing to be on his side or breaking his leg. Siren just made that decision easier. And it was the right decision.

I hate him.

I hate him for marrying the most incredible, badass woman and then cheating on her. He's probably the reason Siren is cold as ice and incapable of feelings. He's the reason she was willing to hurt me. He's the reason she's working for Julian. I hate him for letting her be sold like property to another man. I hate that he hurt her. I hate that by hurting her, he threatened any hope Siren and I have of being together.

I hate it all.

Siren got to take her vengeance out on him; now it's my turn.

Hugo is still writhing on the floor in pain. He turns his head and spits blood mixed with his own tears.

God, he's such a baby. How could Siren ever fall for a man like him?

Hugo and I are polar opposites. He's thin and lanky. His hair is light brown. His eyes are bright blue.

While I'm hulk-like, with dark hair, and a scruffy beard.

He's clean-cut.

I'm a broken ship with more scars than perfect skin.

There is no way one woman could love us both. Even at different times in her life.

She likes a man like Hugo, maybe not one that cheats, but the perfect looking man. And I'm not him.

It makes me even angrier.

"Get up," I say.

Hugo wipes the blood from his nose on the back of his hand.

"Get the fuck out, and call a nurse," he demands back.

Tsk, tsk.

He should learn to follow my orders faster. He's not the one in charge here. *I am.*

"Get up," my voice booms with the full force of my anger. Shaking walls and telling every person in this hospital that I'm in charge of everyone and everything.

Hugo immediately scrambles to his feet.

"Sit," I say, calmer this time, knowing when to use my powerful voice and when to hold back.

Hugo sits.

"Good dog," I say.

"I'm not a dog."

"Aren't you? You do whatever Julian says, just like his obedient dog would. You don't have brains of your own."

"Like I told Aria, I didn't have a choice. It was follow his orders or get shot."

"Hmm, that sounds like you made the wrong choice. No one hurts Siren and gets away with it."

"Siren?"

I don't answer him.

Instead, I lean forward and look him in the eyes. "Now, you are going to answer my questions, and I won't break your other arm."

Hugo looks like he wants to hit me, but he won't. His

muscles are thin compared to my bulk. He wouldn't have a shot against me. And at the same time, he also looks like he's about to cry at the thought of having his other arm broken.

"I'll tell you whatever you want. I really do hate Julian Reed. You didn't have to send your bitch in to do your dirty work so I was weak before you talked to me," Hugo says, sending dirty looks to Siren, who is still sitting in the corner of the room watching us like a hawk. I have no doubt if Hugo tried to lay a finger on me, she'd jump in to defend me, just like she did with Julian.

With Julian, she was ordered to do it. *With me, though?* I'm not sure why she keeps protecting me and hurting me. She's a conundrum.

"I didn't send her. We aren't working together. She handled her business with you; this is about you and me."

Hugo rolls his eyes. "Get me some pain pills, and I'll tell you whatever you want to know."

"No, tell me what you want to know, and I won't break your other arm, that was the deal."

He huffs. "What do you want to know?"

"What does he want with my boss, Enzo Black?"

"What he always wants, control and money. Mr. Black is the most powerful man in these oceans. He wants to take him down and take over his business."

"How much does he know about me?"

"Just that you used to work for him. He thinks you know everything about Mr. Black and that when he is finished using you, he'll be able to use you to trade you to get what he wants from Mr. Black."

"He thinks he'll get control and money in exchange for me?" That doesn't make sense.

"I guess," Hugo shrugs. "He doesn't tell me his entire

plan or why, but I assume he wants a weapon or something from Mr. Black that can help him become more powerful."

"Siren, go get us those pain pills. Hugo's been a good boy."

Siren eyes me suspiciously, but she leaves. Giving me a minute, two at the most, before she returns.

"How does Julian know about Lucy?"

Hugo's eyes light up. It might have been a mistake to ask him when he can use the information to hurt Siren. But I need to ask. I have to protect her. And I vowed to stop protecting Siren. This is me keeping that promise.

"Aria."

My eyes fall. *Siren knows about Lucy? She was the one that found out about her and betrayed her to Julian?*

That can't be?

But when I look at Hugo's happy grin, I know it's true. And he just destroyed all of the relationship I've built with Siren. We are officially over. It's one thing to hurt me. It's another to hurt an innocent woman.

9

———

SIREN

I DON'T KNOW why Zeke sent me out to get pain pills. I know he isn't going to give them to Hugo.

I suspect it's because he wants to ask Hugo something without me there. And I don't know if it's because he's hiding something from me or if he thinks Hugo will answer more honestly without me there.

But loving someone is about trusting them. And the only way I can earn Zeke's trust in return is by showing him that I trust him.

So I go and get the damn pain pills from the nurse.

And when I open the door, I feel the shift in the air. Zeke's pissed, and Hugo is happy as a clam.

Hugo's eyes find mine when I enter the room, as if to say he's won. I just don't know what the fuck he won or what he's talking about. But it doesn't feel good.

I shouldn't have left. Now wasn't the time to prove my loyalty to Zeke. Not when I know what scum Hugo is. Zeke doesn't know all his tricks yet.

"Thank you for answering my questions, Hugo. You've

earned your pain pills." Zeke turns to me and motions for me to toss him the pills.

I do.

He catches them with a coldness in his eyes I wasn't expecting to be aimed at me.

What did you tell him, Hugo? Before I left, Zeke and I were basically on the same side. And now, I can't read him at all.

He unscrews the cap and hands two pills to Hugo, who takes them and swallows them dry.

Such a wimp, I barely injured his nose. And his wrist—well, I guess I did some damage there.

"I won't break your other arm," Zeke says.

I hold my breath because I already know what Zeke is going to do. And it's going to be exhilarating to watch.

Hugo grins smugly. *Oh, you idiot.*

Zeke grabs the IV pole and slings it as hard as he can against Hugo's kneecap.

The scream Hugo makes is the most magnificent melody I've ever heard. I'll never forget the sound. It's high-pitched, and agonizing, and everything Hugo deserves. The pain hits him everywhere. His voice, his eyes, his entire body rings with the pain as his kneecap shatters.

"That's for hurting Siren," Zeke says, and I get flutters in my stomach. He hurt Hugo to defend my honor. Just like I hurt Hugo to defend his.

"You said you wouldn't hurt me if I told you the truth, you fucking bastard."

"No, I said I wouldn't break your arm, and I didn't. I keep my word, unlike you." Zeke stands taller. "And I gave you the pain pills even though it wasn't part of our arrangement. Too bad it will take at least half an hour for them to start taking effect. And Tylenol will do nothing to stop the sharp pain in your knee."

Zeke starts walking toward me, but I'm not sure if he's walking toward me or the door.

"Dammit, I should have gone for the kneecap, so much more effective than the wrist," I say, hoping that the joke will lighten the mood.

But Zeke isn't in a playing mood. He's all seriousness. As he passes me, he snaps his fingers, indicating for me to follow.

I want to, but I don't like being treated like his pet. Not by him.

I follow, but I bring my anger with me. Zeke searches the hallway before spotting what he's looking for. He walks to a door that has a janitor's sign on it. He pops the lock with a quick thrust up of the door handle, and then he opens the door, holding it open for me to step inside.

I study him carefully, trying to figure out what happened in the two minutes I was gone to get the pain pills.

"You first," I say, needing to take back a sliver of control.

He growls, but I don't back down. Not until he tells me what's going on.

After a quick staring contest, where neither of us back down, Zeke steps into the dark closet. Only then do I follow.

The door shuts behind me, leaving all light outside the dark closet. I'm sure there is a light switch, but neither of us moves to find it.

The closet is small, so small that we are face to face, and I can feel his breath on my cheek.

I try holding my breath, not willing to give him any pleasure until he talks to me. But he doesn't hold back. He's angry. *With me.*

Well, good, I'm angry with him. For shutting me out. For not letting me talk. For not letting me spend every second kissing his face and riding his cock.

He can be pissed at me and still fuck me. We are too good together not to.

"How many secrets are you hiding from me?" His voice comes out strained and wanting.

I exhale a shaky breath, doing everything I can to not kiss him again. I was the one who initiated our last kiss and that got me nowhere. If he wants to kiss me, he's going to be the one to do it.

"Too many," I answer honestly. "How many are you keeping from me?"

"Not enough."

And then his lips claim mine.

The kiss slams me back against the door. It's hard, taking my breath away, but also demanding so much more. It takes my control, my power, my heart. It demands I spill my secrets in order to get more.

But both of us have our secrets, and neither of us will ever tell the whole truth. Because we need to keep our secrets in order to protect ourselves, and more importantly, each other.

Our secrets can wait, though.

This kiss cannot.

My hands wrap around his neck, as his hand grabs my shirt, flinging it off me before I realize that he's trying to angrily fuck me in the janitor's closet.

I don't care; I want this man too much. And I'll take him any way I can get him. Rough, dirty, in the fucking janitor's closet.

My bra goes next, and then his head dips, nibbling roughly on my nipple, making me gasp and squirm against his lips.

"Zeke, fuck."

He smirks against my nipple.

And then his hand is dipping down to my pants. Undoing the buttons and zippers before shimming them down my hips. Then his fingers plunge into my panties, ripping them from my body before finding the wetness between my legs.

Yes!

More.

His fingers tease between my folds but never find my clit. The longer Zeke goes without touching my most sensitive spot, the faster I realize that he is never going to. He's going to take out his frustrations on my body by denying me the one thing that could bring me the most pleasure.

Two can play at this game.

I lunge forward, grabbing at the waistband of his jeans, but Zeke grabs both of my wrists and has them pinned above my head with one hand, while his other hand continues to torture me by rubbing everywhere except the one spot I want him to.

I could fight him. I've done it before. Sure, Zeke is strong and has muscles for days, but I'm smart. I could get out of his hold.

But the striking gaze of Zeke's eyes, even in the dark, tells me that I'd be smart not to fight.

"What did Hugo say?" I ask.

"Really? You're going to bring up the topic of your ex-husband when I'm currently trying to fuck you?" he hisses against my cheek. His breath like fire and temptation and so damn hot.

"But you're not trying to fuck me; you're trying to torture me."

He grips my wrists harder, the weight of his body pressing against mine. Him clothed, me basically naked.

It's hot.

But it's also the angriest I've ever seen Zeke. Something happened. Something I'm missing the pieces to. Something he thinks I did—the worst thing.

But what?

Worst than betraying him to Julian? Worst than not telling him about my husband?

We are both silent for a beat. Both trying to decide what to do next. How to have the upper hand with the other person. But there is no upper hand when it comes to us because there is no us. There is just tension, frustration, and longing. Secrets, truths, and lies. And stories that aren't ours to tell.

"Truth or sin, Siren?" Zeke asks.

"Ask me," I say, waiting for him to accuse me of something that most likely Hugo or Julian did. Because Zeke doesn't trust me, he'd rather trust either of them than me. Even though he knows they are evil. I'm worse.

"How did you find out about Lucy?" Zeke asks.

I blink—once, twice. Racking my brain for the information he seeks. The information that has caused him to pin me naked in a janitor's closet. The information that has him more pissed than anything I've ever done before.

"I don't know who Lucy is," I answer.

He laughs. "Stop lying! For someone who says they can't lie, you sure do it all the time."

"I'm not lying! I have no clue who you are talking about." Although, I'm desperate to know who he's talking about. *Who is Lucy?*

He growls, low and beast-like. The sound is half-anger and half-need.

"Tell me or I get to commit a sin," Zeke says.

The threat is meant to intimidate me. It's meant to scare

me. I'm vulnerable, pinned naked against the door. I'm completely at Zeke's mercy.

Except I'm not. I could escape if I wanted to. And as much as Zeke hates me, he isn't like Hugo or Julian. He won't really hurt me. He can't without hurting himself.

There is nothing Zeke could do to me. But he could do it to someone else. Drag a nurse into the closet to fuck and make me watch. That would be the only torture I couldn't stand.

"Truth or sin, what did Hugo tell you?" I ask, needing to get the complete picture from Zeke.

"Truth—Hugo said that you were the one who told Julian about Lucy. That's three times you betrayed me. And it will be the last."

I swallow, holding back tears. Because there are no words that can make Zeke believe that I not only have no idea who Lucy is, but I didn't find her and turn her over to Julian. And right now, I can't prove to him the truth.

So I only have one option.

"Sin," I say, and I know it's what Zeke wanted me to say. He didn't want me to tell him the truth. He didn't want me to defend myself. He wanted me to give him a reason for him to be cruel. He needed a reason to show me how pissed he is.

"Wrong choice," Zeke says, and then his mouth comes down hard on my neck. Marking my skin with his lips, his teeth, his hungry growls.

The move isn't meant to bring me pleasure; it's meant to treat me like he owns me. He doesn't know that no matter the reason, having his mouth against my skin is hot as hell.

I feel my body come alive again with hope that Zeke will finish what he started. That he'll fuck me. And inadvertently make me come.

But that wouldn't be a sin.

I moan, accidentally letting him know how much I enjoy him kissing my neck hungrily.

"You like that, babe?"

Babe? He never calls me anything but Siren. And I hate any other name falling from his lips.

"What about this?"

His hand reaches between my legs, and if I was wet before, now I'm drenched. Because unlike last time, he finds my clit, confirming that he knows exactly what he's doing when it comes to my body.

"Fuck, Zeke," I moan as I hump his hand. Knowing that at any moment, he could stop and leave me unsatisfied. Leave me wanting, desperate to come without a release.

"Yea, baby? Just like that. You're so close."

I am. I'm so fucking close.

And then he stops. His hand disappears from my body.

So...so close!

Dammit.

My eyes open, and my body ices at the loss of pleasure.

Zeke smirks.

"Last chance, tell me the truth, and this will all be over."

"You wouldn't believe the truth, even if I told you."

"You're right; I wouldn't."

Zeke jerks my hands down and spins me around, before pinning my hands behind my back. Again, he's holding my wrists with just one hand—as if that is enough to contain me. The move might work with most women, but not with me. I could break free.

But Zeke needs to punish me. He needs to hurt me for something he thinks I did. Even though I didn't.

But if letting Zeke take out his pain on me just this once helps him heal, I'll do it. I've destroyed this man enough.

And I can take it. Whatever he has planned can't be as bad as what I've gone through with Hugo and Julian. Or even before as a kid.

"I choose sin, Zeke. So far, all you've given me is mild amusement," I say, goading him a little.

He doesn't take the bait.

"I'm not a cruel man, Siren. So don't twist things around and make me out to be one."

Siren, I'm back to Siren.

"Then stop acting like one," I say, hating that my voice sounds small and scared and timid. It doesn't sound anything like me.

Another lie to myself, because Zeke most definitely can cruelly hurt me. Only he has the power. Saying he doesn't is a lie—one of the biggest.

He doesn't answer. Instead, I hear him unzip his jeans.

And I tense waiting for the intrusion. Waiting for the delicious stretch. Waiting for him to drive inside of me with all of his fury.

Instead, his hands release my wrists. I stand hunched over my ass in the air. Waiting. But I realize, I'm waiting for nothing. Because Zeke isn't going to angrily fuck me.

He moans.

Slowly, I turn and see Zeke jacking off to my naked body. And I realize what his sin is. He's going to come, but I won't. He'll use my body to get off, but he won't touch me. He won't help me come.

I consider touching myself to the sight of Zeke pumping himself. It's a glorious sight. One I know I'm going to have dirty dreams about later. And I want nothing more than to come with him.

But I want to show Zeke that I'm not a monster. I want to

show him that I'm on his side. That I would never hurt this Lucy person whoever she is.

So I don't.

Zeke's eyes heat when I turn, and he gets a clear view of my body. My nipples hardening under his heady gaze.

I want him so badly.

But he won't let me have him. Not right now. Maybe never again.

He pumps furiously, taking his anger out on his cock since he can't on my body. He wants to come fast. End this quickly. And I have just the idea to help him.

I kneel in front of him, his eyes gaze at me in a curious way, but he doesn't stop or ask what I'm doing.

My lips are level with his cock. And I know what I want, but I'm not sure Zeke will let me.

But his eyes haven't left mine, and I know he's trying to figure out what I'm doing. This is my chance to touch him, to get to taste him. If I can't have him how I want, then this is the next best thing. Giving him pleasure and stealing some for myself.

I lick my lips and then open my mouth wide. My eyes turn sultry, telling him exactly what I'm willing to do.

He groans, still pumping with his hand, but he can't resist. And he won't deny himself the pleasure of a blowjob.

He glides his hand over his cock one more time; his cock grows another inch in his hand as it somehow hardens more at the prospect of my lips wrapping around him.

And then he inches forward, pushing my lips wider as his cock slides between them.

I smirk around his cock, feeling victorious. And then he starts moving in my mouth, hard and fast, trying to punish my mouth while he chases his orgasm.

He thinks he can hurt me this way. He doesn't know I

don't have a gag reflex. He literally can't hurt me this way. *But I can hurt him.*

I let my teeth scrape against the ridge of his thick cock, and he gruffs, his eyes shooting me a warning.

I smile and then wrap my fingers around him in addition to his cock. He stills, letting me do all the work as I pump over him.

Each thrust of my hand and lips earns me another moan. Each deeper, louder, and stronger than the previous. Each telling me that he's seconds away from exploding in my mouth.

He started with all the control here, but I took it. I demanded it.

His body begins to tense as his orgasm nears. I consider dragging it out, making him wait and torture him like he tried to torture me, but I won't. Because I want to taste him. I want to know that I'm the one who made him come.

The only one.

Except I'm not. *Who has made this beast of a man come before? How many others?*

My thoughts made me hesitate, and Zeke shoots me a look as if to say, 'if you stop now, I'm going to kill you.'

It does the job, and I'm quickly back to driving the man crazy with my lips and hands.

My other hand reaches up and strokes his balls as I take Zeke all the way in my mouth and down my throat.

His eyes widen, and his mouth parts as the most wonderful throaty sound pushes from his mouth.

Say my name. Say it.

I push him further over the edge. He's so damn close. I never want this to end, and yet, I want everything. I'm greedy like that.

I swirl my tongue over the tip, before plunging him deep

in my mouth again. And this time, the tidal wave that is Zeke explodes in my mouth. He fists my hair as he comes hard into my throat. And then I wait for the sound I've earned after the blow job I just gave him.

Instead, I get...

"Yes, Lucy!" Zeke screams, destroying me.

I didn't think he could hurt me. *I was wrong.*

With one word, he cut me down.

With one word, he punished me more than any man could.

Lucy.

If I didn't know who Lucy was before, I do now. She's the woman in his life. The woman he loves. The woman he'd do anything for.

And I just let him use me while all the time he imagined her.

I swallow and then wipe my mouth on the back of my hand before I gather my clothes, throwing my shirt on quickly and angrily.

Zeke doesn't speak. But he stares, judging my reaction to what he just did.

I grab his T-shirt off the floor and throw it at him.

"Ask Julian," I snap at him.

"Ask Julian what?" he asks.

"Ask him how he found Lucy. Because it sure as hell wasn't me." And then I storm out, leaving him in the damn janitor's closet of the hospital I hate for so many fucking reasons. This moment just added one more. I'm never stepping foot in this fucking hell hole again.

And I'm never thinking about Zeke again. Not as a friend. Not as a lover. I'll protect him only because by protecting him, I'm getting him the fuck away from me.

I storm outside, ignoring the stares at my tears and half-dressed appearance. When I go to jump in the Corvette I drove here in, I remember I illegally parked, and the car has been towed.

So much for a quick getaway.

And then I see Zeke walking out to his truck, and my heart aches. Once again, I lied to myself. I may hate him, but I still love him. And I'm going to make him pay for making me feel both.

10

———

ZEKE

I screamed Lucy's name.

Lucy!

A woman I haven't thought about in years.

A woman I haven't envisioned naked in decades.

A woman I haven't dreamed about since I was eighteen.

A woman who would slap me if she knew I had called out her name during sex with another woman.

I'm an asshole.

Worse.

I'm a jackass, a dumbfucker, a cunt. I'm every curse word you can think of.

I'm also a man.

A dumb, stupid, idiotic man.

I had only planned on jacking off to the sight of Siren. I planned on denying her what she wanted—*me*. I planned on coming on her magnificent tits. And then leaving her to clean up her mess.

Instead, Siren kneeled down in front of me with her big eyes and plump lips, offering me what every man in the world wants. And I couldn't say no.

Literally couldn't.

My brain said to tell her no. But my body, *damn, I didn't have a prayer against her.*

The longer she licked, pumped, and tasted me, the more I lost control. All of it. I gave it all to her.

Siren knew exactly what she was doing when she knelt in front of me. It may have looked like she was surrendering to me, but bloody hell, she was taking all of my power.

Thrust after thrust.

Deeper into her throat I sank. Until she completely controlled me, and my sin became more of a surrender than a threat to cause her pain.

We've been locked in this twisted game of truths, lies, and sins since the moment we met. We've been playing even before I came up with the exact rules of the game. We've been playing for a lot longer than that.

And I couldn't lose.

Not when she struck me where it hurts the most—*Lucy*.

So in my moment of haze, the last moment before I gave her everything, I came up with a plan to keep my power—a stupid plan. One I regretted the second her name fell from my lips.

Lucy deserved better.

Even Siren deserved better.

I should have let her won. I should have known that I could win the next round.

But I was beyond pissed. I thought that in the moments we've spent together since Siren told me she was married that we've made progress in our relationship. That we've moved beyond the hate and found our way to somewhere new. Somewhere where we wouldn't lie and hurt each other.

I was wrong. Because it is all part of Siren's plan. To wreck me, destroy me without ever laying a finger on me.

I walk outside the hospital, vowing never to return to this horrible place. A place where I do stupid, cruel things I regret. Although, I don't regret breaking Hugo's kneecap. That was rather fun to hurt the man who married Siren and made it impossible for me to ever claim her.

And then I spot her.

Siren is standing on the sidewalk with her phone in her hand and no Corvette.

It got towed.

Which means she's either waiting for a cab or me.

She hasn't spotted me yet. I could sneak off to my truck and drive home without having to face her. But I figure the least I can do after calling out another woman's name while her lips where wrapped around my cock is to offer her a ride home.

Home.

I don't even know where she considers home.

My house?

Julian's?

Does she have her own house somewhere on the island? Or does she share a place with Hugo?

Just another secret that Siren keeps from me.

I walk over to my truck, still deciding what to do. If she rides back with me, the car ride is going to go one of two ways. Either we will sit in awkward silence the entire time, or we are going to have a fight that's going to lead to me wrecking my truck and us fighting until we both fall off a cliff.

I unlock the truck and get in. And then I'm backing out of the parking spot before I realize what I'm doing.

What am I doing?

I drive to Siren standing on the sidewalk waiting for a

cab, that on this island will take a good half hour or more to get here.

I lean over and pop the passenger's side door open without a word, commanding her to get in the truck.

She hesitates for a single second, and I swear her eyes are glistening with moisture.

A sure sign of tears that she's desperately trying to hold back.

Tears I don't understand.

She can be mad, *sure.*

Angry, *absolutely.*

But sad? *No way.*

She can't be sad about what happened. She can't be emotional. She's the least emotional person I know. She doesn't have a heart. I guarantee when she said yes to marrying Hugo that it was a calculated move. She thought she would get something out of it.

But then she's climbing into the passenger seat and slamming the door shut like she wishes my balls were trapped between the door.

There's the anger I expected.

I nod and wait until she buckles her seatbelt before I take off. More to make sure she's contained to her seat and can't reach over and strangle me than for her safety.

I start driving; neither of us speaks. Apparently, we are going with the awkward silent treatment the whole drive.

Which sounds like the better of the two options.

Until I realize there is a third option.

I flick the radio on. The radio stations are limited here. And there is more Bob Marley on the radio than anything else.

But the song currently playing is the rare non-Bob Marley song. It's 'Before He Cheats' by Carrie Underwood.

It's a song about heartbreak and how the woman plans on making the man pay for what he did.

Siren doesn't miss a beat. She starts singing along until her voice overtakes the artist singing. Until she is all I hear. Until I know I won't be getting her voice out of my head. It's beautiful and haunting and so damn mesmerizing.

"Zeke! Watch out!" she screams.

I slam on the breaks just in time to avoid hitting a stray chicken. But the car spins at my sudden stop. I step harder on the breaks, forcing the hunk of metal to stop just inches from the damn chicken that Siren was so worried about saving.

I huff, out of breath.

Siren grips her seatbelt as she stares over the front of the dash. "Is it alive?"

The chicken takes the moment to flap its wings and jump forward out of the road.

You couldn't do that thirty seconds ago?

"Yes, it's alive. But we almost weren't," I growl as the truck is also inches from slamming into a palm tree.

"Because you are the worst driver ever!"

"I was driving just fine until you had to get all noble and try to save a chicken. A fucking chicken! It's a bird you eat for dinner, and you seem to have no problem with that. Yet you were desperate to save the chicken when..." I huff, ending my sentence on mumbled words instead of the truth. That she cares more about a chicken than she does me.

Siren doesn't have to hear the end of my sentence to know what I was about to say. Somehow she seems to know my every thought before I say it.

"Well, if you behaved better than the chicken, then I would want to save you too," she yells.

All hell breaks loose after that.

"You know, for a second, I was going to apologize for what I did, but then I remembered you are an arrogant, manipulative woman who thinks she's better than me, and now I won't," I say.

"Yea, well, you're an ass!"

"Great comeback."

"Speaking of coming, how was your orgasm? Because it will be the last you will be getting for a while."

"Ha, you wish it was the last orgasm. It will be the last orgasm I'll be getting from you. Not the last one I'll be getting. And thank god for that, it was a struggle to come, what with you slobbering all over me." *It was sexy as hell and the best damn blowjob of my life.*

She smirks. "Yea, it looked like you really struggled to come."

"It was very difficult, but it shut you up, so it was worth it. Unlike now."

It's all a lie—every word. But somehow, I can't let her have the upper hand. I just can't.

"Asshole."

"Bitch."

"Bastard."

"Cunt."

"Jackass."

"Siren."

Our eyes lock, and I want to say more. I want to tell her that if she'd just stop lying and trying to ruin my life, I could call her my lover. I could call her my everything. But that will never happen.

A horn honks.

And I realize we've been sitting in the middle of the road blocking the path for far too long.

I turn the wheel and start driving again.

This time, I drive in silence, but it's not awkward. It's horrible really. Because we both keep replaying all the horrible things we've said and done to each other. All the things that ensure we never go anywhere near loving each other again.

There is no love between us, only hate.

Siren's phone rings, and she stares down at it with trepidation, but she answers, which means it can only be one man—Julian.

"Yes," she answers.

There's a short pause, and then she says, "We're on our way." Before she hangs up.

I don't have to ask what Julian said. I know that he summoned Siren and me to his place. And I know why—to discuss the next round of the stupid game. Which means he'll be assigning me another task. The second of five for me to complete. Which means I'll be one step closer to being free. One step closer to returning to my normal life.

Right now, I don't care about the stupid game. I care about getting the answer to one question. *How did Julian find out about Lucy?*

Hugo said it had to do with the sassy brunette sitting next to me. But something feels off. My gut doesn't know who to trust—*Hugo or Siren?*

Julian is the tiebreaker. Not that I can trust him either.

I need to know the answer. I need to know how to protect Lucy. But I have a feeling needing to know how he found out about Lucy has a lot more to do with my feelings for Siren than it does Lucy.

11

SIREN

Zeke drives straight to Julian's house without asking me what Julian demanded.

He knew.

And he didn't argue with being summoned.

I don't analyze why. My focus is on something else entirely.

When Zeke pulls up in front of Julian's house, I'm out of the truck before he's even put it in park.

I don't wait for Zeke. In fact, I want to get as far away from Zeke as possible. Even if it means running toward Julian.

Julian spots me when I enter his house without knocking. He raises an eyebrow when he spots my angry snarl.

"Don't wait for me to start," I say, running upstairs, not waiting for permission from Julian.

I head down the hallway to what I know is a spare bathroom—a bathroom no one ever uses.

I shut the door carefully and lock it even though I know no one is coming after me. No one is going to check on me. Because no one loves me. No one could ever love me.

I'm too ruthless.

Too cold.

Too heartless.

Too determined.

Too strong.

Too callous.

Too everything.

I don't need a man, or at least that's the persona the world sees. And therefore, no man needs me. No man loves me.

I slump to the floor in front of the door.

And then I cry.

Big ugly tears.

Tears that turn to sobs.

Tears that consume me.

That rattle my entire body.

That shake the door.

Tears that ruin the mascara on my face.

Tears that turn my eyes big and puffy.

Tears that cause snot to run down my face.

Tears that pour out of my eyes until they begin to burn.

I've never cried over a man, not until Zeke Kane.

When I saw Hugo in bed with another woman, I didn't cry. I was angry; boy, was I angry. But I didn't cry. I was strong.

But Zeke is a man worth crying over. I cry so long I'm not even sure why I'm crying anymore.

Sure, him calling out another woman's name hurt. But it was intentional, not an accident. He didn't mistake me for Lucy. He knew exactly what he was doing—*hurting me.*

And he succeeded.

Not because of his stupid game. Not because he said her name. But because I realized who she is to him.

He loves her. Or at least did.

Lucy has what I will never have—the love of Zeke.

I've hurt him too many times to earn his love. And I'm too self-reliant to ever depend on a man, even Zeke.

I don't want a boyfriend, definitely not a husband.

That's what love requires—a commitment.

Something I will never give. Something I will never have.

I will never experience love. Not real love. The kind where the man loves you as much as you love him. The kind that makes you do stupid things like get married and have kids. I will never have that kind of love. Not because I'm not worthy, but because I know what love does. Love destroys. And I refuse to spend the rest of my life crying on the floor because of love.

But when I stand up, clean my face, and try my best to cover up my puffy eyes with the makeup I find in the drawer, I know that I'm lying. Because I still love Zeke. He's the man for me. Even if he doesn't think I'm the woman for him.

Even though we continue to hurt each other, my heart is his. And I'd rather have it shattered by Zeke than loved by another man.

12

ZEKE

"STOP PLAYING GAMES," I say as I enter Julian's sitting room. The room he prefers to do his business in. The room that contains more cigar smoke than actual oxygen.

"Hmm, I don't know what you are talking about," he says, pouring three glasses of scotch even though Siren disappeared upstairs and has yet to return.

"Sure, you do." I snatch one of the glasses and take a sip.

He eyes me. "Nope, no idea. I've kept to my side of the deal."

"I'm talking about Hugo Martinez."

"Oh, you mean Aria's husband? Yea, I heard he had a horrible accident and ended up in the hospital."

I glare. "He had an accident all right—took a swing to the nose, a wall to the wrist, and an IV pole to the kneecap. He'll be in the hospital for at least a week while those heal, I suspect."

Julian's eyes widen at my admission. Apparently, Hugo hasn't told him what happened.

"Sounds like my Aria," he says, assuming she was the

one to deliver all the blows. I don't correct him. I'm not the kind of man to break a bone and tell.

"About Lucy," I start.

Julian just shakes his head. "Aria will be down soon, and then we can talk."

I frown. Julian just wants Siren here when I ask about Lucy. He's trying to play games. I don't like it.

My ears strain, trying to listen for Siren. Siren disappeared up the stairs on a mission the second she stepped foot in the door. *I have no idea why. Could she not get far enough away from me fast enough?*

Or did it have to do with something else?

Julian and I wait in silence, mostly glaring, trying to intimidate each other.

But with each second that passes, I grow more uncomfortable. *Where is Siren?*

I consider going to look for her, but there is an unspoken rule hovering between Julian and me. Neither of us will go look for Siren. Neither of us will show weakness for a woman that we have both fallen for in different ways. A woman we both despise, while respecting how incredible she is. A woman we both want to be ours.

So we stare, our eyes doing the talking our mouths won't. Each of us confident we are going to win this battle between us and win Siren over to our side.

"What are you two doing?" Siren asks as she struts into the room, instantly warming the room with her heat.

"Waiting for you, my pet," Julian says with a knowing smile.

She shoots him a dirty look before grabbing the glass of scotch he poured for her and sitting in a chair between Julian and me.

"I told you not to wait for me," she says, avoiding my gaze and looking at Julian.

"We didn't think it would be polite to start without you," I say. *Look at me, dammit!*

She doesn't.

"Did you get whatever was so important taken care of?" I ask.

She nods into her glass, still not looking at me, which only piques my curiosity more.

Suddenly, I notice all the changes in Siren—they're subtle. I don't think Julian sees them, but he also hasn't spent all day with her like I have.

Everything is slightly different. Her hair was pulled back, but it's now let down, dangling in front of her face like a shield over her face. Her jeans and shirt have damp spots on them. Her face looks like she's reapplied makeup, as her face is a shade brighter than before.

She takes another sip of her drink, this time, her hair falls back, and her eyes cut to me for the briefest of seconds. And then I see the real difference—her eyes.

Her eyes are red—both of them. Just enough for me to notice something is wrong, but not enough for her to be getting sick. The puffiness around her eyes stands out, even though she's mostly hidden it with her caked-on makeup.

And then she sniffles. Just once, but it's enough.

Enough for me to know what she's been doing upstairs this whole time—crying.

Why?

Because of me?

Because of her situation?

Hugo?

Almost dying in the car?

I've never wanted to read her mind more than I do now.

I've never wanted Julian out of the picture so I could scoop her up in my arms like I want to now. I want to know who made her cry for almost an hour upstairs so I can hurt him like I did Hugo. Even if that bastard is me.

Instead, I'm forced to sit in my chair and act like I don't notice her eyes, her sniffles, her heart breaking.

But the way her eyes study me noticing her, she knows that I know. And I swear I see moisture gather in the corner of her eye at that thought.

"Ready for round two?" Julian asks.

"Yes," I hiss impatiently.

He grins. "You don't have to act all impatient about it. You have four rounds left. It can be all over today if you just answer each question honestly instead of choosing sin."

"Ask your question," I say, refusing to acknowledge him. If I was selfish and just wanted off this island, I would answer all of his questions. But I'm not selfish. I protect my friends. I protect Lucy.

"Where is Mr. Black's vault?" Julian asks.

Fuck, he knows everything. Everything I've vowed to protect for so long. Julian Reed knows.

"How the fu..." I start, but Julian's dark glare stops me. I can't make Julian know how secretive the vault is and how impressive it is that he knows about it. He can't know that it's important.

And yet, without me speaking, he already knows. He knows how crucial it is. He probably knows what the vault contains.

Fucking christ. How does he know?

Siren.

She's being incredibly silent during this conversation. Her eyes are buried in her glass, not lifting to look at me.

Because she was the one who found out the information

about the vault. She was the one who found out about Lucy. I'm sure of it. She might have even met Enzo Black before.

I don't trust her, but *god, that doesn't stop me from wanting her.*

"Sin," I say, knocking the rest of my drink back, praying like hell that this task he gives me will be easier than the last one.

"Since you won't give me the location of the vault, I want something equally as valuable as what I would find inside," Julian says.

"And what would that be?"

"One billion dollars."

I scoff. "You have plenty of money. What do you need that kind of money for?"

"None of your business," he answers.

"Fine, I agree to the deal, if you stay away from Lucy. She is no longer part of your negotiations."

His smile curls up. "No. Lucy is very much part of our negotiations. You may not love Siren anymore, but you love Lucy. I found your weakness, and I promise to exploit it."

Siren looks at me now. And her eyes say everything. That she had nothing to do with finding Lucy. *Why would she, when the mention of her name slices into her heart as easily as a knife?* Siren wouldn't help Julian find a woman from my past, not when it impeded her ability to control me by being the only woman in my life. I see the pain in Siren's eyes. Pain at the mention of me loving another woman.

I do love Lucy, but not in the way Julian is saying. And definitely not in the way Siren is thinking.

But I don't let either of them think differently. I keep my mask on like a protective armor.

"Lucy stays out of this," I say firmly.

"No, you finish your five tasks or answer your five questions honestly, and I won't touch Lucy. Just like I won't touch Enzo, or Kai, or Langston, or Liesel. Not until the game is over. Afterward, they are all fair game again. But you'll be free to go and protect them."

FUCK!

My choices are to drag this game out into eternity to ensure Julian never goes after my friends, or spend this time learning everything I can about Julian, so when the game is over, I can defeat him.

Or find something he wants more than Enzo Black. Something to keep my friends safe.

"Aria has my bank account information. I don't care how you get the money or who you steal it from. I want that amount deposited to my bank account by the end of the week."

I open my mouth to argue. To yell. To say I would never get him that kind of money.

"Lucy is doing great in Seattle, by the way. The rain and coffee life suits her," Julian says, standing and walking out the door, dropping a bomb to ensure I do exactly as he says.

Enzo Black is strong. His empire is formidable. I've done my best to protect him so far. I never want to bring an enemy to Enzo's doorstep. But if I had to, I would, knowing Enzo would destroy them.

Lucy is different. I can't bring an enemy to her. She doesn't belong in this world. It's like Julian knew I'd grow tired of his games. That I'd grow tired of being away from my friends. That soon, I would give up defending them, and I'd run to their side, preparing them as best I could to defeat Julian. Lucy was his ultimate bomb drop. He knew he could control me as long as he had access to Lucy.

She's in Seattle.

She's probably living a happy, unsuspecting life in the

city. Julian mentioned coffee, and I can very much see Lucy loving that town. She loves coffee. I can imagine her being an excellent executive at the newest coffee roasting company. She wouldn't settle for anything less than being an executive.

Siren stares at me while I'm thinking about Lucy. And I finally realize what the tears she cried earlier were about. Because I see the look now on her face. A look that says her heart is shattering right in front of me.

But why?

Siren doesn't love me. She doesn't even care about me.

There is no way she can be feeling anything other than jealousy at me thinking of another woman.

But that's not what my eyes see. And that's not what my heart feels. And whatever Siren is feeling scares the shit out of me.

13

SIREN

"I'll meet you at your house in an hour, and we can discuss a plan," I say.

Zeke stands, like he can't get out of the room fast enough. It would make sense if it were Julian he was running from. But he's not running from Julian; he's running from me.

"How are you going to get back?" He pauses in the doorway.

I don't look at him. I can't, not without breaking and showing him just how much he means to me. How much I love him. How I know he'll never love me back.

I stretch. "I have two feet. I'll walk."

He doesn't say anything else, but I feel his presence leave the room. And I don't know if it ends up more gloomy with him gone, or if the fog lifts when he leaves.

I wait a moment, trying to decide what I want to do. Trying to figure out what Julian's plan is.

But Julian Reed is a complicated man. He doesn't tell me his thoughts because he doesn't trust me as much as he wants me to be his number two, I'm not there yet. Not in reality.

I could let Julian destroy Lucy, get rid of my competition, so to speak. But I can't stand to watch Zeke shatter. I love him. And that means doing the right thing, even if the right thing means sacrificing myself in order to save the woman Zeke loves.

I stand up and pour myself another glass of scotch, shooting the glass of liquid down my throat for courage to go do something that someday is going to lead to a broken heart.

And then I go in search of Julian, who is, of course, nowhere to be found on the main level. His car is still in the garage, though, which means he's in his bedroom. The one place in this house I feel completely uncomfortable in. Julian knows that.

Fuck.

But I'm not going to let the fact that I have to talk to him in his bedroom stop me. I'm on a mission. A mission to save Zeke's girl.

Zeke's girl—what I wouldn't give to earn that title myself.

The door to Julian's bedroom is closed. So I knock. I'm not about to walk in on him indecent or fucking another woman or touching himself. That's exactly what Julian would want.

But of course, it doesn't stop Julian from opening the door shirtless. He's wearing his dark dress pants and no shirt.

His body is nice. He has abs and hardness in all the right places. He has a slim waist and wide shoulders. But I guess it's the evil heart and wicked eyes that stop me from pining after him in any way. It's hard to be attracted to someone after you've seen them kill someone just because they fucked up and brought you the wrong food. *A big turnoff, trust me.*

"Yes?" Julian says, his eyes telling me to ogle his body like he's doing to me.

"We need to talk."

He holds the door open, and I step inside, ignoring his perfectly unflawed body. Unlike Zeke and I's body that has been marked with bullet wounds, with knives, with scars, Julian's body is perfect. Because he has people like me who do his dirty work, so he never has to.

"You breaking up with me, Aria?" Julian asks at my choice of words.

I wish—I wish I could break up with Julian, but somehow, I keep finding myself more and more in debt to him.

"What will it take to ensure that you never go after Lucy?" I ask. I don't even know her last name. All I know is that Zeke needs her protected. So I'll protect her with my dying breath. I'll do anything. I can't pretend I wouldn't. I need to try to manipulate Julian into trading Lucy for a simple task I can do for him.

But Julian knows me too well. He knows I have a thing for Zeke. Worse—he knows I'm in love with Zeke. He was the first to know, even before I realized it myself.

Julian shakes his head in disappointment. "I thought you were better than that. Are you really going to keep loving a man who will never return your feelings?"

I don't answer that. Because I am better than that. I am stronger. *And no, I don't plan on spending the rest of my life loving Zeke when he's in love with someone else.* But from the outside looking in, I've hurt Zeke so many times. If I can do something to mend the bonds I've broken between us, then I will.

I put my hands on my hips, staring Julian down, refusing to talk to him about my feelings.

"What will it take?" I ask again.

He stretches, and his pants hang lower on his hips. *Gross.*

"Let's see," he rubs his chin, pretending to think. But he already knows what he wants. It's the same thing he's always wanted—me in love with him.

He's never raped me, except for the one time he came close. He's never taken it because he wants me to offer myself to him willingly. The only thing I've offered is my loyalty. My skills are working in his favor. That's the best he's ever going to get.

"Julian," I hiss my warning.

He cocks his head. "Aria Torres."

Chills surge through my body, and not the good kind. If Julian calls me anything other than his pet, he always uses my real name—*Aria Torres.*

No one else calls me that. Not Nora, not Hugo, and not Zeke.

Sometimes I feel like the only person I can truly be myself with is Julian. He's the only one who knows everything about my past. He's the only one who can see my true feelings because he's desperate for me to turn those feelings towards him.

"What will it take for you to leave Lucy alone? For you to tell me where she lives so I can make her disappear? So you can never find her again?"

"Don't you mean so Zeke can never find her again?"

"No." I'll tell Zeke where she is. Even if it will kill me to see him run to her.

"You're getting better at that lying thing, Aria."

I frown; he's noticed. I'm so close to being able to lie out loud that it scares me, the temptation of it. Because if I can lie, I can be in control again. Right now, I've only been able to lie to myself.

"But you aren't there yet." Julian sighs. "You know most people see you as the devil's right-hand woman. But you are every bit an angel."

"An angel that can murder you and sleep peacefully right after."

He grins. "That sounds like the very definition of an angel to me."

"You're stalling."

"Am I? I guess I'm just hoping you seeing me shirtless in my bedroom will give you ideas. Especially since that oaf doesn't know a good thing when he sees it."

"This was a mistake," I say, turning and pretending to walk out. I know the second that I rescind his ability to strike a deal with me, he'll gravel. He likes our arrangements. He likes keeping me close.

"Wait!"

I smirk but then let my expression fall when I turn around. "Yes?"

"Agree to a date."

"What?"

"Go on one date with me, and Lucy is off the table."

My eyes widen—he's serious. I thought I would have to trade years of my life to protect Lucy. I thought I would have to do something big. Something huge to keep her safe. But all he's asking for is one date. One single date.

And somehow, one date seems like the worst thing he could ask for. A date with the devil, not exactly thrilling. But not the worst he could ask for.

"One date. Two hours. No kissing."

He puts his hands in his pockets with a grin. He looks like such an innocent boy, not the horrible serpent he is.

I hold out my hand to make the deal. "And no sex."

He sighs. "No sex, not unless you agree."

"I want her address, now."

He pulls out his phone and types something before handing it to me.

I study the Seattle address until I have it memorized.

I sigh. I don't know who Lucy is, but her life just got a lot more complicated. Even though I trust Julian to keep his promise to me, I know Zeke won't. Which means I have to make her disappear. Get her to a new place, with a new identity. It means I have to tell Zeke where she is and that she's safe.

It means Zeke will be one step closer to realizing I have feelings for him—true feelings.

And it scares the shit out of me.

Because I don't want him to know the truth. The truth will kill me. The heartbreak will end me.

I'd rather pretend I'm a strong, unbreakable woman— the independent, calculated siren.

Instead, I'm just a woman who fell in love with the wrong man. Then I fell in love with the right man, but it was too late. Because the right man hates me. The right man is in love with another woman. The right man will never love me back.

I hold my hand out again until Julian's hand meets mine. I've made deals with him before for love—but this time, I know I got the better end of the deal. One date to save a life is nothing, especially when it means saving Zeke's love.

"When?" Julian asks.

"Tonight, I want to get this over with."

14

ZEKE

I open the door after the petite knock barely makes me aware of the presence of someone at the door.

I assumed it was Siren, and she was timid after talking with Julian. But when I open the door, it's one of the last people I expected.

"Nora, what brings you to my door?" I ask, hesitantly.

"Aria texted and said you were going to be in need of a plane and wondered if I could help," Nora answers, pushing past me into my house without waiting for an invitation.

I rub my neck, not having a clue what to do with Nora while we wait for Siren. I'm not the best at being friends with women. At least not the kind who wear dresses and makeup and don't have a clue how to hold a gun—women like Nora.

Women like Siren, like one of my closest friends, Kai, who belong in this world and wield a gun as good as the rest of them, that kind of woman I understand.

"Siren isn't here right now," I start, but notice Nora has already made herself at home with a beer in my living room.

She's flipped the TV on, something I haven't had time to watch since I've moved here.

I brace myself to watch one of those redecorating shows or reality TV shows, but instead, she flips to a soccer game.

"You like soccer?" I ask.

She nods. "I lived in England for a while, and I fell in love with soccer."

By the way her eyes are following the men's asses on the screen, I'm not sure if she fell in love with the game or the men. Or both.

But I grab a beer and sit on the couch next to her, hoping the game is enough to distract me while I wait for Siren to get here so we can make a plan on how to steal a billion dollars. I'm not bad with security systems, but I've never stolen that kind of cash before. So I'm hoping Siren has a better plan than I do.

Because my plan is to shoot Julian in the head, and hope none of his men kill Lucy before I can get to her. Which is a stupid, idiotic plan. Not one I will be able to risk. I won't risk Lucy's life.

I feel her before I see her. Of course, Siren let herself into my house.

"Don't you have a house of your own?" I ask, my eyes leaving the TV for the first time in an hour.

Nora glares at me, thinking I'm an idiot for asking.

But Siren just sighs. "No, I don't have my own house, actually. I have a room at Hugo's, a room at Julian's, and here. I would sleep at Nora's, but she still lives with her parents in Anguilla, and just sleeps in hotels when she comes here. So no, I don't have a house. And I'm sorry if I prefer your house to Hugo's or Julian's, but I don't have a lot of choices."

I swallow. *I made a mistake.* I realize now that I'm not even sure if Julian pays her with money for the job she does.

I clear my throat. "Do you have a plan?"

"Of course," she responds, but she doesn't look happy. Nora and her exchange a glance, and it looks like they've had an entire conversation I'm not privy too.

"So, where are we going? Who are we stealing from?"

"France," Siren answers.

"Okay? Who's in France?"

Siren walks down the hallway to the bathroom.

"Hugo's parents," Nora answers.

We are stealing from Hugo's parents. "His parents have that kind of money, and Siren had to sell her soul instead of them helping their son out when he got in a bind," I put together.

Nora nods solemnly.

Siren pops her head back in. "Do you have a dress I can borrow?"

"Nope, I'm all out of dresses," I answer.

Siren rolls her eyes.

"Yep, I brought one in my bag," Nora answers.

Siren nods.

I look at her closely. "You really want to steal from your in-laws?"

"Don't you?" she asks.

"Well, yea...but I just thought..."

"Trust me, I've wanted to steal from them for a long time. If Hugo is an ass, they are the hole he came from."

Nora runs off and returns a moment later with her bag. She starts digging through it and tosses Siren a black dress.

"Are we going tonight? Is that why you're getting dressed up? Should I change?" I ask.

"No, we aren't going tonight," Siren grabs the dress and disappears down the hallway.

I follow after her and catch the bathroom door before she closes it.

She bats her eyes at me as if waiting for me to leave so she can change, but I'm not going to. She's hiding something from me. If she's planning on crying in the bathroom again, I want to know about it.

I open my mouth to ask her what happened and why she was crying, when she throws her T-shirt off over her head and starts undoing her pants.

Yep, there goes thinking about anything other than her body.

I should go. I shouldn't keep looking at her when she's undressing. But it's too late. There is no way I can walk away now. Not from a mostly naked Siren.

"Why aren't we going to France tonight? Wouldn't it make more sense to fly overnight so we can sleep on the long flight?" I ask, finding my words somehow, even though I'm sure my mouth is gaping open as I stare at her.

"Nora can't fly us all the way to France in her little propeller plane. She can fly us to Miami, and then we can catch a flight from there."

Miami.

I stare at her, devoid of emotion. She knows Miami is Enzo's base of operations. *Is this a ploy to get me there and then use me as bait for my friends?*

If it is, she's a very good actor, because she gives me nothing.

"So, we can't fly tonight?" I ask.

"We could, but the flights to France usually don't leave until the evening. We wouldn't make it to Miami before the flights leave for the night. We will have to wait until tomorrow."

Her words make sense, so I try not to read too much into them.

And then she unhooks her bra, and I watch with wide eyes as it falls to the floor at her feet. But I'm not looking at her feet. I'm looking at her perky breasts and pointed nipples. She totally knows she has me under her spell. There is no hiding how I feel in response to seeing her naked body. My reaction is immediate and intense. My cock pushes hard in my pants against the zipper, desperate to have my way with her again.

My brain shouts *never*, while my cock screams *aways*. And my heart—that asshole has sped up at the beautiful sight of her, and it wants to give her another chance. We've already given her two! Two chances, and both times she hurt us.

Her breath catches at my response. She grabs the dress off the vanity and slips it over her head in one quick motion like she wasn't just standing in front of me, baring her gorgeous tits to my face.

She reaches behind her and pulls up the zipper in one motion. This is Siren, and she never needs a man's help. I can no longer breathe because Siren is standing in front of me in the tightest fucking black dress. It barely covers the important parts of her. The dress belongs to Nora, who is a good half a foot shorter than Siren.

She flips her hair back, and I realize now why she can't wear a bra with the dress.

I'm drooling, staring at her breasts in the dress that accentuates her curves, and her nipples are just visible enough beneath the fabric to be sexy, but not overtly.

She looks damn good in that dress.

She turns away from me, running her hands through her hair to fluff it. Then she's searching for the drawers of my bathroom until she pulls out a couple of makeup items. Makeup she must have stashed in here earlier.

She starts applying red lipstick, and that's when I come to my senses.

"Siren? Why are you getting all dressed up?" *And why don't you want me to get dressed up?*

Her eyes cut to me out of the corner of her eye, but she finishes applying her lipstick and looks at herself one last time in the mirror before she turns to me, as if she knows that when she answers, she won't be continuing to apply makeup.

"I'm going on a date," she answers.

I take a deep breath as she hasn't said with whom yet. *Hugo? Or me?*

Since Hugo is in the hospital with a broken wrist and kneecap, I doubt it's him.

And since I'm standing here not in date attire, I doubt it's me either.

"Hmm, and who is taking you on a date?"

She bites her lip. "Julian."

I lose it. "Julian? You mean the asshole who has you trapped in a contract for ten years? The asshole who is blackmailing me into turning over my boss to him? The man who is slimy and evil and killed innocent men? That man? The man I thought you hated?"

She nods.

"So let me get this straight. It wasn't enough that you are married and have been fucking me, but now you want to date Julian? How many other men are you sleeping with?"

Her face turns red. "How many men am I fucking? Really? That's the question you care about?"

"Yes," I growl. I care. I want to know just how big of a slut she is. I want to know what number I am on her list among many.

"None! I'm not fucking anyone. You were the last man I fucked, and hell will freeze over before I do that again." She tries to move past me out of the bathroom, but my large frame is blocking the way.

"Move!" she gruffs.

"You really are a slut, Siren. You'll spread your legs for any man if it means you get something in return."

Shit, I may have taken things too far by calling her a slut. But I'm pissed. It was one thing to learn she had a husband. Even one she doesn't love. It's another thing to learn that she also wants to date Julian, the most vile man on the planet.

Her eyes water in anger, sadness, shock. *Yep, I definitely took things too far.*

"You're an ass," she says, shoving me hard against my chest, pushing me back out of her way so she can escape the bathroom. She struts to the living room with me right behind her.

"Yea, and you're a slut," I say, doubling down on my insult. I don't think I've ever used the word against a woman before, but heartbreak will do that to a man. Make you lash out in any way you can to prevent the pain.

"Shoes," Siren says to Nora, who is sitting on the couch watching our exchange wordlessly. Nora reaches into her overnight bag and pulls some strappy black heels out.

Siren snatches them and starts putting them on while still standing. That's how much of a hurry she is to get away from me. Not that I blame her, I want to get away from her. She starts walking toward my front door with her shoes halfway on.

Just as she reaches for the door, I slam it shut, caging her in with my hands.

"Why?" I whisper, taking my anger down a notch. Maybe there's an answer, an explanation. My voice pleads for there to be a good reason for her to be getting all dolled up to go on a date with Julian. But for the life of me, I can't come up with a reason.

She closes her eyes as if to shield herself from me.

"Why are you going on a date with Julian?"

She reaches for the door handle again, and this time, I let her open the door. I'm not going to force her to tell me the truth, not anymore. If she has a good reason she wants to share, she'll tell me.

And then I see them, the glistening tears against her cheek.

"I'm doing this for you. To keep your precious Lucy safe." She walks out the door, slamming the door in my face, leaving me alone with my stunned expression.

"You really are an ass," Nora says from behind me.

I agree, the biggest.

"Come on, let's make some popcorn. I have a feeling we are going to be up all night worrying about our girl," Nora says, taking pity on me.

But I can't turn to follow Nora. Instead, I keep looking at the door and the expression on Siren's face. It was the truth. She's going on a date with Julian to protect Lucy. She's doing it for me.

Why?

The answer is obvious. But I'm not ready to go there again. I'm not ready to risk everything. I'm not ready to be vulnerable. But I do know that I'm going to be staring at the door all night long, desperately waiting for Siren to strut back through it.

It's just a date.

Exactly—it's a date. So I don't know why I expect her to

be walking through my door again tonight. She'll be spending the night with Julian. She'll spend the night in his bed. Or at least his house.

I may have gotten Lucy back, but I just lost another woman—Siren.

15

SIREN

THIS DATE IS by far the worse date I've been on, and I've been on some doozies. Dates that ended with a drunk man puking on me, getting left with a two hundred dollar bill, and even an attempted drugging. But my date with Julian Reed tops them all.

And I can't even tell you why exactly, just this strange feeling in my gut that says Julian is up to something. *He's always up to something.*

Because as much as Julian has wanted to control this date, he isn't. *I'm in control.*

At first, he tried to fight back, but I quickly took control, and I haven't let him have it back since the moment he tried to pick me up in his fancy Aston Martin. He opened the passenger door and expected me to sit obediently, but instead, I slid all the way into the driver's seat.

After my little fight with Zeke, I needed the distraction that driving offers. And I couldn't stand for Julian to drive. I needed to feel in control.

It continued when he tried to hold the door open for me; I took it and waited for him to enter first. When he tried to

104

order my drink for me, even though he ordered my favorite, I asked the bartender to bring me a different one. When he ordered my meal, I ordered another.

The date became one big fight for control, one I was definitely winning. However, Julian didn't seem too upset to be losing.

I was winning—until now. I feel the brush of Julian's fingers under the table against my knee.

I freeze. I can't stand to be touched by this man. By any man really, but especially this man. The only man I want touching me is Zeke. And right now, I don't even want him to touch me because his touch reminds me of everything that we will never have.

Julian's hand slides up my thigh.

"What are you doing?" I ask, gritting my teeth to keep from yelling at him in this posh restaurant.

"There was nothing in our rules that said I couldn't touch you."

His hand slides higher, hitting my limit.

I grab his middle finger and twist, getting that instant release of pressure as I dislocate his finger.

Julian's face scrunches in pain for a split second, and then his face goes neutral.

Huh. Maybe he has a higher tolerance for pain than I thought?

"It wasn't part of our agreement because I didn't think it was necessary to state that you weren't allowed to touch me. You are never allowed to touch a woman without her expressed permission."

His eyes darken as he leans forward. "You want me to touch you. I can see it in the way your lips part anytime I talk, hanging onto every word I say. I can see it in the way you keep crossing and uncrossing your legs. The way your eyes grow heavy with lust. You want me."

I take a deep breath, and then I dislocate his ring finger. This time he doesn't even cringe. He was expecting me to hurt him.

"Well, let me clear some things up then. I don't want you. I don't like you. I hate you." I release his hand and fling it back in his direction. "Don't ever touch me again."

"You can say whatever words you want. They are all lies. You may not even realize it yourself. But your body doesn't lie to me. Your body wants me, even if your mind doesn't."

I shake my head. "My body wants Zeke, that's who I've been thinking about all night."

It's true. I've been thinking about Zeke all fucking night! Been thinking about our last kiss. Been thinking about the taste of Zeke's cum between my lips. Been thinking about how great angry fucking against every hard surface in the house would be, but it isn't going to happen. Because Zeke doesn't understand. He will never understand why I make the decisions I do. Why I outwardly betray him, while secretly protecting him from greater evil than he even realizes exists.

Julian shakes his hand and then carefully pops each finger back into place.

Excellent—now I can dislocate them again.

"Zeke will never want you like you want him."

"You don't know that." *Even though I know it's the truth.*

"I do. You want to know how I know for sure?" He leans forward again like he's about to tell me a secret. And I find myself leaning forward as well.

"I know because you will never like me like I like you," he says.

I frown and lean back before taking a sip of my Pina

colada. *Yes, I ordered a frozen Pina Colada even though this is a restaurant where you only order wine or scotch.* I also ordered macaroni and cheese off the kid's menu—anything to make this less of a date and more awkward for Julian.

"That's because you are an evil monster who would feed his child to the wolves if it meant you got ahead in this world."

He nods. "Exactly, and Zeke thinks of you in the same way. He thinks you are a selfish cunt who only cares about herself. He doesn't know what you've done for him. He'll never know. Even if you told him, he wouldn't believe you."

I suck on my straw until I get every last drop of the frozen drink that's more sugar than alcohol into my mouth. Julian's right. Zeke will never want me. Never like me. Definitely never love me.

But it doesn't change my feelings for him, at least not right now. Maybe when he's gone, and he takes my heart with him, will I realize that loving him was a mistake. Right now, it feels right. Like I was put on this earth to love Zeke. To protect Zeke.

Zeke may think I'm a siren luring him to his death. But he got it right the first time—I'm his guardian angel watching out for him, he will just never know that I'm an angel in disguise.

"Don't give up hope yet, though," Julian says out of nowhere.

My eyes flicker up hesitantly, unsure what he's saying.

"I thought that was exactly what you were saying, to give up hope. Because it's the same lost cause as you trying to go after me. It's never going to happen."

He drinks down the rest of his scotch. "The odds are against us both. But every once in a while, a man picks the winning lottery numbers, gets struck by lightning, and hits the game-winning three-pointer. It doesn't happen often, and sometimes the results are worse than the current life. But it happens. It can happen. Rarely, and unexpectedly. But our lives aren't about the expected."

I swallow, afraid of the words that are coming next.

"You have three men who want you in different ways. Three men who have carved their names into your neck. Three men who have wanted you. And by the time this is all over, you'll end up with one of us. Hugo, Zeke, or me. You're destined to."

"What if I want to run away and live a normal life with a normal man? A man who is a teacher or lawyer, a man living a sane life, one where I don't have to carry a gun with me everywhere I go."

He smiles gently. "Because you don't want that life, Aria. A teacher's life is boring. And a lawyer can be just as corrupt as I am. And don't for one second pretend that you don't enjoy carrying that gun. It gives you power and control over your life. Something you desperately want."

He's right. I like the gun. I like using my skills. *But what if I want more? What if I want something different? Something that isn't just shooting and killing people? And fighting?* Sometimes I'm tired of fighting.

But I'm not tired of this life. I just want my partner to carry on the fight when I can't. When I'm too tired to fight. When I need a break.

Julian's right that I can only ever be with a man from this world. I can't start over with a plain, normal, and boring man. I need a man who can fight as well as I can.

Hugo, Julian, or Zeke.

But the only man for me is Zeke.

"Have I fulfilled my dately duties? Are we finished?"

"Just about."

Julian stands and motions for me to do the same. He guides me out of the restaurant with his hand on the small of my back.

I'm going to make him pay for the gesture. For the burning touch that I can't do anything about without making a scene in front of all these people. The second we get to the car, all bets are off. The date is over, and I can do whatever I want.

The valet has already pulled the car around without us having to ask. Julian is a regular at this restaurant. It's also why he never handed them his credit card. They already have it on file.

The valet goes to open the passenger side door for me, and this time, I don't fight Julian for the driver's seat. I want a few minutes to be lost in thought before we get back to Julian's compound, and I have to decide between finding a guest room in Julian's house to sleep in or going to Zeke's. Neither seems like a great option right now.

Julian drives wordlessly back to the compound, but he doesn't stop in front of his house. He stops in front of Zeke's. As if he knows that's where I'm headed. Or he wants to make Zeke jealous or angry by him showing up with me.

He put the car in park.

"Deal over? You won't touch Lucy?" I ask.

"I won't touch Lucy. You have her address and information, and I'm guessing you already have a plan to move her elsewhere."

I don't answer, but he knows me well enough to know that it's exactly what I'm doing.

I grab for the door handle, when Julian grabs my face and turns it toward him until our mouths are inches apart.

My eyes fly open, and red warning bells go off everywhere.

And without thinking, I have a gun pointed at his temple.

He grins at my reaction but doesn't release my face. Probably because he knows I won't kill him. If I do, Lucy is dead. And so is Zeke. He has fail-safes in place to ensure Zeke and I don't kill him without losing something we love as well.

"This date is over, Julian. I agreed to one date. No kisses. No sex."

He nods. "The date is over."

"Then, what are you doing?"

"Offering you a second deal."

I close my eyes. *Don't listen. Whatever it is, it's not worth it.*

"I'll trade a kiss for time."

"Time?" I ask, keeping my eyes closed. *Don't fall for his tricks. Don't fall for the devil's schemes.*

"When the game is over. When Zeke has finished his last task or answered his final question, I'll be free to chase down his boss. I'll be free to kill them all, Zeke included. I'm trading one kiss for one day. I'll wait one day, give Zeke a one day head start to return to his friends and try and keep them safe. One kiss for one more day of Zeke getting to live instead of dying. One kiss for one day."

Damn him. He already knows I'm going to accept. I would do anything to keep Zeke alive. I would give Julian anything to ensure Zeke has the best chance of survival. And in this game, one day can mean everything.

"Deal," I say, keeping my eyes closed, keeping the tears at bay. *It's just a kiss.*

A kiss Julian will play in his head over and over. A kiss he will dream about. A kiss his thoughts will stray to when he's masturbating. A kiss he will think means so much more than just a kiss.

I wait, unmoving, for him to kiss me. My heart thuds wildly, not from excitement, but from trepidation. *I can't do this.*

Zeke. *Think about Zeke.*

So I do, and I realize that is what Julian is waiting for—for my mind to go somewhere else. For him to be able to kiss me without the pain, for him to kiss me when I'm most vulnerable.

His lips press against mine, and his hand cradles my head and neck, keeping me from ending the kiss too soon.

We didn't talk rules of the kiss.

How long?

Are tongues allowed, expected?

Nothing.

I'm a passive participant.

I let him kiss me, but I don't kiss him back, even with Zeke flicking in my head.

Julian puts everything into the kiss. He spreads my lips, his tongue dips and swirls in my mouth, and his throat gives off soft moans.

I feel nothing but sticky lips against mine.

Finally, he releases me. And his eyes heat into devious slits.

I've never understood why Julian hasn't just forced me. *Why hasn't he raped me if he wants me?* I'm sure he's raped other women before. But with me, it's his favorite game. To try and convince me to choose him. Only then will he have his way with me.

I don't know why. *Does the man think he loves me?* I doubt Julian Reed is capable of love. But then, most creatures are. They just love in different ways.

Julian shows his love by not raping me.

Zeke shows his love by protecting me.

And I show Zeke my love by betraying him to keep him safe.

I step out of the car wordlessly. I walk up to the front door and knock, unable to push my way into Zeke's house when I was just kissing Julian.

When Zeke opens the door, I know he saw the kiss. If his anger was a ten before, now it's a hundred. The ensuing battle is going to be one of our most intense.

16

———

ZEKE

Siren went on a date with the devil to keep Lucy safe—a woman I've led Siren to think I love. A woman who means the world to me, but not in the way Siren thinks. I'm not in love with Lucy; I just love her. She's part of my life, my family, my world. And I will do everything to protect her.

And it seems, Siren will too.

I stare at the door Siren just left through, unable to get passed what just happened. I'm angry. And happy. Confused and blind. I feel warm and cold.

"Here," Nora thrusts a drink into my hand, but I don't register if it's alcohol or not. Or even what kind.

I just sip.

"What is Siren doing?" I ask, needing to understand who Siren is.

"Isn't it obvious?" Nora replies.

No, it's not obvious. Nothing Siren does is obvious. She's manipulative and selfish and unkind. She's the exact opposite of everything I've ever wanted in a woman. And yet, I'm still here standing in front of the door, regretting letting her go on a date with my biggest enemy.

113

I take a drink and then spit it out. "What the hell is this?"

"Apple juice."

I raise an eyebrow at Nora. "Why the fuck are you giving me apple juice?"

"Because you need a clear head when Siren returns, not be drunk off your ass."

"And apple juice is the way to do it? Why not water?"

She bites her lip. "Because I thought you were too focused on Aria to notice I wasn't serving you wine or alcohol."

I shake my head. "I'm not focused on Siren."

"Then why are you standing in the foyer staring at a door? She's going to be gone a least a couple of hours; you should sit in the living room and finish watching the soccer game with me."

"No," I answer, not giving her more of an explanation.

Nora doesn't push me, though.

"You two are so fucked up that you belong together, you know?"

I frown, still staring at the door, memorizing every dark spot, flaw, and scratch. "No, I don't know. We are so fucked up, we are completely wrong for each other."

She laughs. "Want to make a bet?"

Finally, I look at her. "I don't bet on people's hearts."

"What about your own?"

I turn back to the door.

"I don't want your money. I just want you to realize that you've already fallen. It's all wrong. You are both so wrong for each other. You're both toxic to the other. But you're also the cure."

"That's not possible."

She smiles, knowingly. "I've known Aria for years. At the time, she was with Hugo. In love with him, so to speak. It might have been love, but it's not what you two have. When Hugo and her would walk into a room, they didn't demand attention and change the feel of the air like you two. Depending on how connected you two are, you turn the room cold as ice or hot as fire. The two of you together control more than just each other; you control the whole dammed world. And together you can save it or destroy it. Whatever you two have is that powerful.

"Call it hate. Call it love. Call it fate. You were destined to be together. For a moment in time or forever, I don't know. But together, you can inflict so much pain or save so many. But only together. Apart, you are fated to destroy us all. Your pull is too great. Stop fighting it. You don't have to love her, just be with her. Stop letting your jealousy and pride get in the way."

"What about *her* pride?"

Nora shakes her head. "Aria doesn't have any pride. She's selfless."

I snort. "Then you don't know her very well. Or at least you don't know Siren."

Nora gets in my face, her petite body barely coming up to my chest. But she stands on her tiptoes, demanding my attention. "No! *You* don't know her."

Her words shake me. Her words, combined with Siren's actions, have my head spinning. I realize I don't understand anything. And I'm further from the truth than I've ever been.

Nora goes back to her TV watching until eventually, I hear her snoring on the couch. While I stay in the foyer, watching the damn door, willing Siren to come back. To explain what the hell is happening.

Hours pass or days, no idea which. But I see Julian's Aston Martin in my driveway, and I feel like a protective brother ready to pummel his ass for taking my sister on a date.

But when I see him press his lips against hers, any thoughts of her being my sister vanish. She's so much more. She's nothing like a sister to me. Not even a friend.

She's mine.

I don't know what I want with her yet. *To protect her? To love her?* But I do know one thing I want from her. And one thing I want her to keep from every other man.

I want her. I want to fuck her. And I want her to fuck me and only me. I want Siren. I want to make her mine. And I want her to stop being around other men who complicate things and cause me to want to break through the door in jealousy.

But then Siren is out of the car, knocking on my door. And I think I imagined it. Until I see Julian smirking at me through the window. He kissed her. Probably because of me. To play me and manipulate me.

Fuck him.

He may have gotten the date and the kiss, but *whose door is she knocking on? Whose house is she going to sleep in? Whose bedroom is she going to get fucked in?*

I stare at him darkly, and Julian realizes his mistake. He got the kiss—while charming and delicious and everything. I get the girl. Siren doesn't want him; she wants me.

She can pretend to be impartial to the men in her life. But it's me she keeps coming back to. It's me whose cock she seeks. It's me she wants in her life.

Siren is mine, not his.

As I open the door, I make a plan to demand her fidelity once and for all.

Siren walks in silently. Her eyes avoid mine. Nothing on her body tells me she even sees I'm here at all.

I hear the flicker off of the TV in the other room and assume Nora is coming to greet Siren. But she must be making herself scarce instead of coming to meet her friend, because she never appears.

"Truth or sin?" I ask.

"Sin. I'm tired of talking," she answers, willing to play even though she won't fucking look at me. Won't acknowledge my presence.

"Wrong choice," I say, getting her attention before my mouth claims hers. When I say claim, I mean claim. My mouth devours her lips, demanding everything from her.

At first, she doesn't kiss back. She's stunned. I don't know if she's still turned off from her earlier kiss with Julian or if I surprised her by kissing her. But the tension she left me in for three hours caused this—this explosion of want and need and desire.

I don't think she's going to kiss me back. I don't think I'm going to be able to convince her to sin with me.

But then she kisses me back. Her tongue presses between my open lips, hesitantly asking for what she wants instead of taking it. It's all the opening I need.

I grab her neck and kiss her with everything I have, sweeping my tongue deep into her mouth, telling her how much I want this. Need this. Demand this.

Her tongue doesn't accept mine; it fights back. We battle for control, for space, for air, each of our tongues viciously dancing with each other. And then it's not just our tongues fighting.

It's our entire bodies.

We battle to rip at each other's clothes. My hand is slipping under her dress, hiking it up over her ass.

Hers reach beneath my shirt, pushing it up as her nails trickle over my abs.

The force of which we battle, limb for limb, causes us to stumble into everything. We dent the wall as I crash her body into it. She pays me back when she shoves me into a glass table, shattering it. Next goes a vase, then a lamp.

We continue to dance, unspeaking. The heat of her kisses does strange things to my body. Somehow her breath alone heats my entire body. All of my muscles contract begging to put all of their energy into Siren. It's making her mine.

She rips my shirt open, and then I rip her dress as I push it higher up her body until it's around her waist.

Her body controls me entirely. She put a lot of effort into manipulating me and my feelings, but all Siren had to do to control me was strip naked, and I would have done whatever she wanted. Her body controls me that much.

Then her teeth bite down on my ear hard, and I suspect she drew blood.

I growl, and that one sound is enough for me to find my voice.

"You traded a date for Lucy," I say, it's not a question. I realized what she was doing. Why she went on a date with Julian, what she meant by she's doing this for me. *For Lucy.*

"Yes, she's safe now," she says, her eyes saying *I don't have to work for Julian anymore. I can run. No one will hurt Lucy. I just need to decide on a plan and leave.* There is nothing keeping me here.

My deal with Julian only keeps my friends alive for so long. But the end result will be the same. I'm just helping Julian get more information he needs to kill my friends while simultaneously trying to get information on Julian for my friends to kill him. But in the end, it's all a wash. I should leave, that's what her eyes say.

I should.

I absolutely should. If I trusted Siren, I would. But I don't. I don't trust that Lucy is safe. Not until I hide her away from everyone, including Siren.

Her eyes read what my mouth won't say. There's a glimmer of disappointment in her eyes, before she grabs my face again and kisses me hard, nibbling on my bottom lip to help ease her sorrow from the thought of me doubting her.

I growl and moan as she tugs, hoping it's enough for her to forget that I don't trust her. We don't need to trust each other to fuck each other.

She must agree, because two seconds later, she's grabbing at my jeans trying to get them undone, and I have her dress up around her arms.

She lifts them, and I pull the dress over her head before I slam her into the wall. And then I see the gun she hid beneath her dress around her thigh.

My eyes go big at how she always keeps me on my toes.

I hold her arms against the wall as I kiss down her body. The sweet curve of her neck, the swell of her breasts, the flatness of her stomach, the soft muscle of her thigh. I undo the strap holding her gun to her leg, and unload the gun while I kiss the inside of her thigh, earning a moan from her. Her eyes never leave mine as she watches me remove the bullets and toss the gun away.

"My turn," she says, turning me and slamming me into the wall like I did her.

She unzips my pants roughly and shoves them down, grabs my gun and tosses it aside with a smirk.

She found my weapon, but I've yet to find all of hers.

I only carry one gun unless I know I'll need more, but Siren carries multiple. While I rely on my size as a backup, she relies on multiple hidden weapons. Although it really should be the reverse, because she has something I don't—

the ability to manipulate, coerce, and taunt others into doing what she wants them to do.

"Where is your other weapon?" I ask.

"Why would I tell you?"

"Because you want me to fuck you, and I won't as long as you have a weapon on you."

"It hasn't stopped you before."

"Yea, and I about got my balls cut off because of it. I won't make the same mistake again."

She rolls her eyes, but reaches into the sole of her heel and tosses a knife aside.

We stare at each other. Her topless, wearing her black thong and heels. Me in only my boxer briefs.

Both of us breathe hard.

Both with completely fucked up hair.

Our backs bruised from being shoved into objects.

This is the moment we make a decision. *Do we cross the line again? Or do we stop?*

Do we talk instead?

We each have several thoughts going through our heads.

Siren wants to know who Lucy is.

I want to know why Siren saved Lucy.

Neither of us ask our questions. We're both too afraid of the answers.

Instead, I grab her hand and pull her toward my bedroom. Once inside, I lock the door, hoping Nora found a different place to sleep for the night, because what we are about to do can not be unheard.

Siren looks at me with heady eyes.

I look at her with longing.

Neither of us touch. If we do, we won't stop. Touching feels like losing, which neither of us wants.

But I know how I can win.

I walk over to the nightstand, pull out a condom, and toss it on the bed before removing my briefs and lying back on the bed.

"I'm tired of you not being mine. I'm tired of not getting my part of you. Julian gets your loyalty. Hugo gets your last name. What do I get?"

"What do you want, Zeke?"

"I want you. I want your pussy. I want your fidelity. I want you to fuck me and only me." *I want you to be mine.*

She swallows, looking nervous.

"Fuck me, and we are entering our own deal. As long as we fuck, we only fuck each other. We don't fuck other people. We don't kiss other people."

Her eyes widen, but I don't have a clue what she's thinking.

"Do we have a deal?"

17

SIREN

Zᴇᴋᴇ ɪs ᴀsᴋɪɴɢ for my exclusivity. He wants me to fuck him and only him.

But that's all he wants.

Me to spread my legs for him and no other man.

Easy enough, since I only want to fuck him. But there is just one problem—*I want more. So much more.*

I want to go on dates.

I want to snuggle after we fuck and not worry about whether or not I should leave his bed.

I want breakfast in the morning and long talks in the evening.

I want chocolates and flowers.

I want to go to the shooting range and take Krav Magra together.

I want to go dancing and sing karaoke together.

I want all of Zeke, not just his spectacular cock.

I want him to be mine, and me to be his. But he doesn't talk about making me his. And I can never make him mine.

Zeke still thinks my loyalty is to Julian, and my last name belongs to Hugo. Zeke doesn't realize all he has to do to

122

make me his is ask. Ask for me to be his and then I'd tell him everything. The entire truth, and then he could figure out if my loyalty really belongs to Julian, and if my name really belongs to Hugo.

Zeke isn't offering me any of those things, though. He's only offering one part of him. The part he thinks he can protect from my scheming. The part that I can't hurt.

Well, technically, I can hurt it physically, but he trusts me not to because of the benefits his cock has for me.

Zeke stares at me, studying every expression, every exhale, every everything. When his lips curl up in the corner of his mouth, he knows what my answer will be.

He runs his hand through his long hair that I can't resist, and then he stands...

Fuck me. I run my tongue over my bottom lip. Zeke may not get hurt in this deal, but I sure will. If I wasn't already in love with this man, fucking him constantly, being so close, and yet not getting everything, I will be soon.

I extend my hand like this is a business arrangement.

Zeke holds out his hand.

And we shake.

The sparks fly between our two hands. Zeke feels it too, because we release our hands far too quickly for two people who just agreed to a sex deal.

I watch as Zeke swallows his uncertainty and splays out on his bed again seductively.

I'm so screwed. My mouth waters, staring at his nakedness on his bed. He's waiting for me to take control. *So fucking sexy.*

"Fuck me, Siren. Prove to me you only want my cock."

My panties are soaked at his throaty words. His dark eyes bore into me, challenging me to make this fuck the best fuck of his life. Prove to him that he was right to take another chance on me, even if he isn't risking anything this time. He's kept his heart as far away from me as possible.

He wants this to be memorable. He wants me to give him my best, while he lies back and does none of the work. *Asshole.*

But damn the way he's staring at me, making my body tingle in all the right places, getting me wet with just a look, tells me he's already doing plenty of the work.

I hook my thumbs into my panties and slowly shimmer them down my legs before stepping out of them. I never think undressing with another person's eyes on you is sexy. It's always hard to not look clumsy or ensure something doesn't get caught on a heel or an ear. But the pained exhale I hear from Zeke shows just how sexy me undressing was to him.

I stand tall in my heels and run my hand through my long hair before flipping it over my head to one side. The move earns me another growl.

"You're not acting like a woman who only wants my cock. You're acting like a woman who wants to play with me," he groans.

"I enjoy playing before I claim what I want," I say, strutting over to the dresser, where a glass of water rests. I slowly take a sip, purposefully spilling some onto my chest. Little beads of water run down my breasts over my sharp nipples.

I can't keep this up much longer, or I'll combust. Zeke has me just as needy as I have him.

My eyes flick to Zeke, who has his cock in his fist, stroking himself.

"I guess I'll just have to get myself off," he says, teasing me into giving him what he wants.

I arch my back as I lean against the wall next to his bed.

"My fingers work better than yours at getting me off anyway," I tease back.

My fingers circle my clit, while Zeke strokes his long, thick cock.

Somehow we ended up in another battle. The battle to not seem weak. The battle to prove that we don't need the other as much as they need us.

"Our deal was you'd only fuck my cock, Siren."

"I'm not fucking any other dicks."

"I think our deal includes self-pleasure."

I raise my eyebrows. *He's going to play that way, huh? Fine, I can play that way too.*

"Then the same goes for you. If I don't fuck anyone but you, then you don't either. You only fuck me, not your hand."

His face is in inexplicable pain. His jaw tenses, his throat locks, his eyelids still, and his nostrils flare.

"Deal," he says, releasing his hand from himself.

He must really want my pussy. Or he can't stand to see me get myself off when he wants to be the one to do it.

I want him to get me off.

Why are we battling again?

We both surrender at the same time.

I jump on the bed as Zeke catches my hips, and my mouth comes down hungrily on his. My hips position themselves over his rock hard cock until my slit is sliding over him, begging him to be inside me.

He grabs my hair, pulling my head back and arching my back to keep my clit against his cock.

"Condom," he gruffs.

"Pill, remember?"

We've fucked before without a condom, so I don't know why he's asking now.

The anger in his eyes tells me he won't verbalize his concerns.

Did I fuck Julian or Hugo? Am I clean?

His tip presses at my entrance, so close to getting what we both want, but he won't let himself, not until he has the answer.

But when I tell him, will he believe me?

I doubt it.

I should just grab the condom on the bed. It will get me the result I want faster, but I crave Zeke without a barrier between us.

Liar!

What I really want is Zeke to trust me.

This is a step toward trusting me.

"I only fucked Hugo once when I was eighteen. I haven't fucked him our entire marriage," I say, repeating what he already knows, but with truth in my eyes.

He nods, accepting this as fact.

But we aren't done yet, because Zeke has more questions.

"Other men?"

"There haven't been any other men after you. Not in my bed. I don't want any man but you." My words make me vulnerable, but they are the truth. "We didn't need to make a deal to be exclusive because I've been exclusive this entire time."

He growls huskily, pulls harder on my fisted hair, and brushes his lips against mine. His cock slowly moves an inch into my throbbing pussy.

*So, so, close...*if he let go at all, I could slide all the way home, enveloping him. But I won't, no matter how badly I want to. I need him to trust me, and he won't if I'm selfish and take what I want without giving him his answers first.

There is one last question in his eyes, and this question hurts him.

"I saw you kissing Julian."

Of course, he did.

I know the truth. I know why I kissed Julian; I did it for Zeke. But I'm not sure he's going to believe that answer. It's one thing to go on a date with Julian to help Zeke. It's another thing to kiss him for Zeke.

But Zeke isn't going to let me get away with not answering him. Not this time. He wants the truth, no matter what that is.

"I kissed him in exchange for getting you one day."

He blinks at me, not understanding.

"I went on a date to save Lucy. And I kissed him to give you one day headstart when this is all over to run before Julian starts chasing you."

He growls, and this time he has no restraint. He flips me over, his cock still resting at my entrance but not entering me. We are having a serious conversation, and yet, we are both turned on. Nothing will extinguish our flames except fucking.

"Stop offering yourself in exchange for saving me. I can save myself."

I scoff. "You would be dead if it weren't for me."

"I know," his voice is serious, his eyes wide. "But I don't need your help anymore, just like you don't need mine."

I nod.

"Stop saving me," he says.

"I'll stop saving you."

"No more kissing other men."

I nod, agreeing.

"No more going on dates."

I nod.

"No more spreading your legs for anyone but me."

I nod slower, agreeing.

Finally, his mouth devours mine, a sweeping kiss to remind me I'm his even if he never says the words. What he said was close enough. We get the physical part of each other for as long as we are together. Which, in our line of work, could mean only a day. But if it is meant to only be a day, I'll make it the best damn day.

I roll us over again, to be on top and in control.

"Trust me," I say, *trust me with this.* I haven't fucked any man but him. I'm clean. We don't need a condom.

He starts to nod but then stops, his eyes revealing a sliver of pain again.

"You haven't fucked Hugo, but did Julian ever..." he can't finish the sentence, but the pain in his eyes tells me everything. *Did Julian ever force me to have sex with him? Was I ever raped?*

I shake my head.

"Say it," he says, his voice desperate. He's right; I need to say it. I can lie with a head shake, but not with my words.

"I've never been raped. Julian has never forced me into sex. I've never fucked him. Since we've started fucking, it's only been you."

"Thank fuck."

His hips buck as I slide down on top of him, his cock filling me completely in one thrust.

I grip his shoulders as the fullness consumes me.

Zeke stops thrusting, waiting for me to adjust to his girth.

But I don't want this to stop.

I start rocking over him.

He grabs my hips, helping me move, but keeping our rhythm slow and steady.

"Faster," I cry. We've gone so slowly, I'm going to explode before ever getting to the good part.

He laughs low and deep. "Slow down or this is going to be over way too fast."

I nip at his lip. "That's what seconds are for." I move faster, and his pained breath tells me he isn't in control anymore.

His hands on my hips slide me faster over his cock, no longer holding back.

I ride him hard, needing the release more than I need to breathe. It's been too long since I've felt this man. I shouldn't go a single day without him, not weeks like it's been.

I shouldn't ever have to worry I won't get to fuck him again, but that's exactly what's going through my head. Even though we promised each other our fidelity, we didn't promise each other forever. This can all end at any time. While it lasts, we are only with each other.

"Siren," Zeke's voice is deep and breathy. But it does what it was intended. His voice brings me back to him.

I smile timidly as I move back in rhythm with him.

Zeke's hands slide up my hips to my breasts bouncing over him. He flicks each nipple, making it harder to control myself. He's driving me wild, and I'm going to come from him playing with my nipples alone.

Not yet; I'm not ready. I want us to go at the same time, and Zeke is still a bit away from his impending orgasm.

I grab his hands and push them back, pinning his hands to the bed as I ride him.

Our fingers interlock, along with our eyes, and at least my heart. This moment is so much more intimate than a simple romp in the sheets.

Zeke seems to understand the change, but when I try to

pull my hands free from his, he holds them tighter, not letting me go.

I'm so screwed.

I blink back the tears at all the intense emotions pulsing through me. *I can do this. Just sex. No emotion.*

The task is impossible, though, with the intensity of Zeke staring back at me.

Focus on the mechanics—hips rolling, legs rocking, lick my lips sexily, rub my clit against his steel core.

But the mechanics all go to hell when his voice strains, his eyes roll back in his head, and his orgasm begins.

The effect my body has on his pushes me to my orgasm as well. We both come in an explosive way. A way that's far too big for emotions to not get tangled in.

But I bury those emotions deep within myself as I cry out from the bang of the orgasm racking my body.

My breath is quick and fast, even after my orgasm rolls through.

Suddenly, I realize Zeke is staring at me calmly. Not like I just rocked his world. But like he's studying for a school test he's not sure how to pass.

I frown. "I can do better..." I start. *What am I doing? Admitting the sex wasn't the greatest of my life?* Just because it wasn't great for Zeke, doesn't mean it wasn't great sex.

Zeke slowly untangles our fingers, and then one hand cups my head, while the other pushes at my hips.

And then I'm lying back on the bed, and Zeke is over me, staring at me like I'm the most impossible woman.

"What?" I ask tentatively.

He smirks. "If you think that wasn't the best sex of my life, you're crazy, Siren."

Then he's spreading my legs with his hands.

"What are you doing?" I ask.

"Showing my appreciation for the sex and giving my cock a moment's rest before I fuck you again."

His head dips between my legs, and he begins licking me sultry and slowly, a complete one-eighty from what just happened.

My gasp takes me by surprise. My hands go to his hair, unable to decide between pushing his head deeper into my folds or pulling him back from the intensity of the pleasure.

Then his fingers are inside me, finding that delicious spot and curling around it. I hate to admit it, but I come hard and fast, letting him know exactly what his lips are capable of doing to me—controlling me completely.

He collapses on top of me, his cock beginning to stir against my thigh, promising more after a quick nap.

I close my eyes and let the gentle pull of sleep drift me away as Zeke's naked body keeps me warm. The difference between lust and love eats at me.

This is just lust, not love. At least it's just lust for Zeke. He loves Lucy. He wants Lucy. This is just sex. Something for him to pass the time until he gets the woman he loves back.

But it's hard to distinguish the difference when he starts playing gently with my hair, doing more to my senses than his cock ever could. For Zeke, this may be lust, but for me, it's all love.

"You're mine, Siren," Zeke says.

I smile and feel settled for the first time all night. It may not be forever, but for now, I'm his. And that's enough.

18

ZEKE

WE FUCKED two more times last night, but it wasn't enough to satiate either of us. At some point, she fell asleep against my shoulder, and I couldn't stand to wake her up. She needs her rest for what is coming today. I loved how she felt buried in the crook of my arm; our bodies melding together perfectly.

Has any woman's body ever felt so perfect in my arms?

Not that I can remember. Maybe it's just been so long since I've fucked another woman. It will remain that way, though, because I plan on fucking Siren in every position and place I can come up with while I'm in Julian's debt.

I say 'debt' because I refuse to be trapped here. I refuse to be a hostage. I'm here because I decided to be here. I want to know everything about him, so when my deal with him is over, Enzo and I will enjoy squashing him like the cockroach he is.

Julian thinks he outsmarted me by having a man monitor Lucy, but Siren gave me the advantage back. I need to talk to her about the details of keeping Lucy safe. I may trust that Siren thinks she made a deal with Julian, but I don't trust either of them fully. I need to hide Lucy myself.

You trusted Siren last night when you put your dick in her without a condom.

That's different.

How?

I don't know. It just *felt* different.

But when Siren wakes, her coldness makes it feel like nothing has changed. We don't talk to each other; we ice each other out. We move around each other like we aren't sharing the same space. Like we didn't explore every inch of each other last night.

I decide to leave it. Eventually, we will have to talk. I shower. I get dressed. I pack a bag full of the essentials I'll need.

"Did you pack a suit?" Siren asks, leaning against the doorframe of my bedroom.

"Do I look like the type of man who owns a suit? Especially when I live on an island?"

She smiles. "We'll get you one when we get to France."

I nod, I don't know why I'll be needing a suit, but I'm guessing Siren has a plan. Right now doesn't seem like the best time to argue.

"I also thought you'd want this," Siren walks forward and holds out a piece of paper to me.

I take it hesitantly and unfold it to read a Seattle address with a phone number underneath it.

Lucy.

My heart beats quickly. More for Siren than for Lucy, but Siren definitely misinterprets why, and I don't correct her. I'm not letting Siren anywhere near my heart again. This is just sexual tension between us, nothing more.

"Thank you," I say, holding up the note and memorizing

it before I shred it into tiny pieces. I have no doubt Siren has already committed everything on the note to memory, and so has Julian, but I want that address in as few people's heads as possible.

"I'm going to need to move her," I say, not saying Lucy's name.

"I know."

"And I can't tell you where I hide her," I say. I can't trust her with someone as precious as Lucy.

"I know," Siren answers sadly.

"It's time to go, you two!" Nora hollers from the hallway, ending the tension between us.

I lift my bag, and Siren starts walking toward the door. "Where did Nora sleep last night, anyway?"

Siren blushes. "Um..."

"Siren, where did Nora sleep?"

"When I first got back, she went out on the back deck to give us some privacy. But it got cold, so she slept on the couch," Siren blushes.

"She heard everything?"

Siren nods.

Fuck, I owe Nora all the coffee at the airport for keeping her up last night.

When I walk into the living room where Nora is waiting with her bags, she drags her eyes over my body.

"So how did everyone sleep?" she winks at me.

Fuck. I run my hand through my hair, ruffling it. I need to put it up in a bun, so I don't keep nervously playing with it.

Fuck it. Everyone already knows what Siren and I did last night. I'm the kind of man that owns his mistakes. Or, in this case, the one fucking thing I did right.

I grab Siren and dip her as I kiss her good morning, surprising the hell out of her.

Nora squeals. "I knew you two would end up together! If only you had actually bet me, I'd be rich right now."

"You're already rich, Nora," Siren says when I release her lips. The smile on her face immediately drops as her brain starts working. "But Zeke and I aren't—"

I kiss her again to shut her up. We aren't together. We are only fucking. But no need to shout it to the world. No need for Nora or anyone else to know our relationship. I'm sure we will have to play the happy couple enough in France. It will be more believable if Nora plays along.

There is no way I'm letting Siren out of my sight. She's mine. Pretending to be a couple is the best way to fend off other men. She won't be flirting with other men to steal the money, if that's her plan. Siren seems to understand because she doesn't bring it up again.

Siren picks up her bag, so I pick up mine and Nora's, and we head to my truck.

I flick Siren the keys to my truck, knowing she will feel safer if she drives. However, I get a scowl in return as I get in the passenger seat.

"What's her problem?" I ask Nora before she climbs in back.

Nora shakes her head. "Men really are clueless, aren't they?"

And women are cryptic.

We all climb in, and Siren drives us to the airport in silence.

When we get to the small airport terminal, I head inside to grab coffees while Siren and Nora head to the plane.

I want to grab a coffee for Siren, but since the last time I ordered one for her, I almost got my head chewed off, I decide against it. I just get one for myself and Nora.

"Here's my sorry for keeping you up all night," I say, handing the coffee to Nora, who is already in the cockpit.

She smiles at me as she takes it. Siren is sitting next to her. I don't look at her. But I can feel her scowl, confusing me even more.

"I can sleep through anything. I only heard the beginning part. And knowing my friend was finally getting properly laid made the lack of sleep worth it." Nora winks at me again.

I nod and then head back to my seat. Siren stays in the cockpit the whole flight. I continue to remain out of the mile-high club.

From the snooty, jealous look Siren gives me when we depart the plane in Miami, I think I played my cards very wrong.

"I screwed up somehow, didn't I?" I ask Nora as she departs next.

"Yep," she says, annoyed with me too.

"You going to clue me in as to what I did wrong or how to fix it?"

"Nope."

Ugh.

But as we walk into the Miami airport, Siren becomes the least of my problems.

We are in Miami. The headquarters of Enzo Black's organization. He, or some of his men, could be here in this very airport. Or this could all be a ruse to use me as bait to get Enzo.

But from the way Siren stalks off inside and Nora chases after, it seems that Siren's focus is on whatever I did wrong and not on an elaborate scheme to take down my best friend.

I let out a calming breath, but nothing more. I need to stay on guard. This could all be a trick. Julian could be here.

I find Siren and Nora sitting at a bar—a whiskey in front of Siren and a margarita in front of Nora.

"Isn't it early to be drinking?"

Siren ignores me and finishes her drink.

Nora gives me side-eye.

Apparently, I can't do anything right.

"When does our flight board?" I ask.

"Twenty-minutes," Nora answers when it's clear that Siren won't be answering me.

"I'll meet you at the gate in twenty then," I say.

Nora nods. Siren acts like I'm the plague.

I rub my neck as I walk away, trying to figure out why Siren is so pissed.

It hits me all at once. *Jealousy.*

Siren can pretend she's not a flowers and chocolates girl all she wants, but she is when I'm the man she's exclusively fucking.

I carried her friend's bag.

I let her drive instead of taking care of her and driving myself.

I got her friend a coffee and didn't get her one.

She wants me to do nice things for her, to court her. To act like she's more than just the woman in my bed, even though that's exactly what she is.

I shouldn't treat her like my girlfriend. She can stew all she wants, but she's told me time and time again—it's not what she wants. And I've told her this is only sex.

But it doesn't stop her jealousy.

It doesn't stop me from wanting to hold her hand and buy her all the damn flowers.

I decide against the flowers. Instead, I get her a coffee, and a grilled cheese sandwich, and a cookie for dessert.

When I get to the gate, I don't spot either of them. Most of the plane has already boarded, so my guess is they are already on the plane.

I board and find Nora and Siren sitting together on one side of the aisle in first class, while there is an empty seat for me on the other side.

I give Nora a glare, demanding her seat.

She stands and gives me a protective snarl.

We dance around each other in the aisle until I'm free to take Nora's spot next to Siren. Siren has put headphones in and is planning on tuning me out.

Not going to happen. I don't plan on spending the flight ignoring each other. I plan on fixing this so the long flight can be much more enjoyable.

I lift her tray out of the armrest. This gets her attention.

Then I place her coffee on it. Then her sandwich. And last the cookie.

I look at her smugly, knowing I did the right thing.

"Wipe that smug smile off your face," she says, reaching for the cookie first.

I smile larger. I wouldn't have guessed she's a dessert first kind of girl. Then again, with our jobs, if you don't eat dessert first, you might never get to taste the best part of the meal before a gunfight breaks out.

"Why? This is what you wanted, right?" I reach out to take a bite from her cookie, and she slaps at my hand.

But she's smiling as she eats, crumbs sticking to her lips, and falling into her lap.

Her eyes cut up to the flight attendant at the front, who

has started the safety demonstration. Siren then looks at me with noticeably pink cheeks, and her eyelashes flirting with me.

"Want to finally join the mile-high club?" Siren asks.

I'm instantly hard.

The flight attendant walks by and says, "Seat belt, sir."

My eyes meet hers, and her face is bright red after noticing my erection.

"How long is this flight?" I turn back to Siren.

"Nine hours."

"I think we can handle becoming a member of the mile-high club at least twice on this flight."

Siren licks her lips, teasing me with what I can't have. If I could have her right this second, I would. The moment we are in the air—she's mine. Fuck the fasten your seatbelt sign, or turbulence, or flight attendants. I can't wait much longer than the five minutes it's going to take us to get up in the air to have her.

But then I remember a not so happy thought—this isn't Siren's first time becoming a member. "You ever going to tell me how you got your mile-high membership?"

She cocks her head, giving me a seductive glance as she thinks about the last time she did it on a plane. "Nope."

I growl, but it only makes her smile brighten as she pulls out her phone and pretends to read a book. There is no way she's reading, not when her thighs are clenched together, and her breath is heavy with thoughts about what we are going to do in that bathroom.

I know one thing that's going to happen—I'm going to erase the other guy from her memory so it will feel like the first time all over again.

19

SIREN

ZEKE'S LEGS bounce up and down, and I remember that he's a nervous flyer. At least when Nora is flying us. But I don't think that's what this is about. This is about us having sex in the bathroom.

Something I can't wait for either, but it could still be a while. We have to climb to an appropriate height. Then the pilots have to turn the seatbelt sign off. Then we have to wait for the first group to use the bathroom to be courteous. Then we have to take turns sneaking off to the bathroom without the flight attendants noticing.

"We have reached an altitude of 10,000 feet. It is now safe to use all approved electronic devices...", the flight attendant speaks over the speakers.

Zeke undoes his seatbelt and then mine, before grabbing my hand.

"Zeke, what are you doing?" I laugh at his eagerness.

"If it's safe to use electronic devices, it's safe to go to the bathroom," he grins back, with determination in his eyes.

I roll my eyes. That's not how this works, but I don't

140

argue with him. There is no use. My stomach clenches with need—I don't want to argue either. I can't wait.

The flight attendant is still making announcements on the speaker when Zeke and I pass her on the way to the bathroom. Her eyes are big, and she's about to tell us off when a man in the front row says, "Ma'am, there is a puking infant in the tenth row."

She runs off to take care of the infant. And Zeke and I casually stroll into the bathroom. Zeke latches the door, and we are face to face in the tiny room.

"They really should make these bathrooms bigger," he says.

I smile. "Don't think you have enough space to put on your moves?"

He grabs my hips and pushes his against mine, letting me feel how hard he is. My pussy soaks and throbs, preparing for him, and he doesn't even have a clue.

But the hitch of his eyebrow says he knows exactly what he's doing to my body.

"We have to be fast—" I start, but I'm cut off when Zeke kisses my neck, making me purr.

"Why? I want to enjoy every inch of your body."

"Because...because we have to..." but my mind can't form words anymore. My mind doesn't have a clue why we have to be fast.

Fast?

Slow?

I want it all.

Zeke's hands are working over my jeans, and I know he can feel how wet I am through them. I should make him take them off before the wet spot becomes even more noticeable when we walk back out. But the feel of his hands over my jeans make my purring and groaning louder.

Finally, I get enough oxygen to my brain. "Are you going to fuck me or just tease me like we are in high school or something?"

That gets him moving faster.

His finger dips beneath my jeans so fast I don't even see his fingers move, but I feel them beneath my panties against my hot wetness.

"Holy fuck!" I cry.

Apparently, fucking all last night did nothing to take away my desire for this man. I want him all the time. *All. The. Time.*

And after we fuck this once, I don't know if it will be enough to survive nine hours on this plane without getting to fuck him again.

"You like that?" Zeke growls.

"Yes!"

But it's not fair to be the only one screaming.

I dip my hands beneath his jeans and find his hard cock.

"Siren," he says my name like a curse, which is exactly what I am—a fucking curse.

And then we can't wait. I rip open the button on his jeans as he undoes my zipper. We both push each other's pants and underwear down at the same time, not even bothering to remove our shirts. Somehow seeing Zeke pantless with a shirt is sexy. Everything about Zeke is sexy.

I grab the scrunchie holding his hair up, pull his hair free, and then I put it around my wrist. He looks like the beast at the end of Beauty and the Beast when he's turned back into a man. Just a pantless beast.

God, his hair is gorgeous. I tangle my hands in his hair at the same time he grabs my hips, pushing us together. There isn't much room in this bathroom, so we are both fighting for everything—room, control, oxygen.

The mirror fogs up as our kisses turn to uncontrollable devouring of each other.

We spin, trying to find a way to make the bathroom bigger so we can take each other the way we want to. Our hands sneak between us, rubbing each other furiously, trying to get the other harder, wetter, more turned on, and reveling in the sound of the other screaming our name out.

My back is against the bathroom door, and Zeke lifts my hands up, demanding control as he kisses my neck.

"God, if I had a bed...the things I'd do to you," he says.

I shudder, holding back from coming at the sound of his deep, sexy voice.

His lips curl up as he notices my reaction.

Control—I need control back.

But more importantly, I need Zeke's dick inside me.

I shove him hard, and he stumbles back until he's sitting on the lid covered toilet seat. Not exactly sexy, but neither of us care. We need each other too badly to care about how we are doing it.

I straddle him, and his cock pushes inside me in one stroke.

I grab his hair, holding on for dear life as I ride him up and down, and he thrusts short and hard into me.

Our eyes lock with each other, and this quick romp in the bathroom starts making me think and feel things I shouldn't. Like how I want to find every bathroom, closet, and alleyway in France to fuck him in.

Then he's pushing up my shirt, and his head dips under as he carefully takes a nipple between his teeth. The sharp pain is just enough to alert all my senses.

I come—hard. *Too hard.* I scream his name, completely forgetting that we are in a bathroom on a plane with hundreds of passengers.

Zeke has a devious expression on his face, but then I thrust down on him while yanking on his hair, and he's growling his own orgasm out.

He shakes his head, like he can't believe we just did that.

"How is it that you always end up on top lately?" he asks, kissing me gently. *Too gently.* I like rough, hard, fast Zeke. Not tender, caring, soft Zeke. Not the man who got me coffee and cookies. This version of Zeke is dangerous to my already falling heart.

"I guess I'm just the stronger of the two of us." I wink.

He nips at my bottom lip. "Yep, that's it. It couldn't be that I like watching your tits bounce up and down in front of my face."

I roll my eyes. "Definitely not."

We both stand and take a second to clean ourselves up before dressing.

I reach for the door handle, and then Zeke grabs my face, turning my lips toward him for one final kiss.

"Meet you back here in an hour?" he asks.

I laugh, but I'm desperate to make it happen again.

At least I am until I open the door and die from embarrassment. There is a line of three people waiting for the bathroom. None of them look happy when we exit the bathroom.

"Sorry," I mumble quietly under my breath as we pass them and return to our seats.

"How can three people need to go to the bathroom already? We just took off," Zeke says.

Nora laughs next to us. "You've been in there for an hour."

"No way," I say.

"Yep, the flight attendants knocked on the door twice,

trying to get you two out, but you were too occupied to hear."

I'm going to die from embarrassment. I've survived gunfights. Battles. Disgusting men. Julian. Hugo. But this is how I'm going to die—of embarrassment on a nine-hour flight from Miami to Paris.

Nora laughs. "I'm just kidding. You were only in there twenty minutes."

I grab a nut from the container the flight attendant brought around and throw it at her.

Zeke just frowns.

"Why are you upset?" I ask.

"It's not a funny joke. I think we should go back to the bathroom right now and prove that I can last longer than twenty minutes."

I chuckle and realize all the eyes in our cabin are on us. The women are drooling and panting, wishing Zeke would do to them what he did to me. And the men are either scowling or ready to high-five Zeke for his impressive stamina.

"I don't think you need to prove anything to anyone," I say.

Yet Zeke kisses me hard, his tongue sweeping away any doubt that he isn't the most impressive man on the plane.

When he stops, I don't even care that he only kissed me to show off to the rest of the plane. *That's why he kissed me like that, right?* Because his eyes are looking at me like he's afraid he's going to lose me again. As if losing me, not embarrassment, would be the death of him.

"Can I get you two a drink? Maybe something that will keep you in your seats?" the flight attendant says, apparently annoyed with our little show.

Zeke turns to her, flashing his million-dollar smile that

rarely comes out because he's usually sulking. "Yes, we'd both love a whiskey."

Suddenly the flight attendant is smiling back at him.

What the fuck?

Isn't she upset with us still? Going to lecture us?

Nope—Zeke smiles, winks, and then she's off to get us drinks like nothing happened.

Isn't there something in the rules about Zeke not smiling at other women if I'm not allowed to fuck other men? It seems like there should be.

I slump into my chair and take the whiskey the flight attendant immediately brings back. I sip on it, hoping it will drown out my jealousy.

Doubtful.

This plane ride is going to feel like forever. I'm not going to survive. And if I do, I'm definitely not going to survive what I have planned in France.

If I can't handle Zeke smiling at another woman, how am I going to survive him pretending to be engaged to another woman? *Me and my stupid plans.*

20

ZEKE

SIREN HAS A PLAN, and I don't like it. Not one bit. It's a stupid plan. Not only that, but if she thinks I can actually pull this off, she's insane. She's lost her mind. She knows I'm not a good actor. I don't know why she thinks this is the only way to steal a billion dollars from her in-laws.

Can't we just sneak into the city and hack their bank account or something? Hell, I'd even take robbing a bank at gunpoint over this plan.

Nora seems just as reluctant as she slips a giant engagement ring on her left finger.

"I swore I'd never wear this ring again," Nora says, staring at the sparkler on her finger.

"Why do you still have it if you rejected his offer?" I ask.

"I didn't reject his offer. I said yes, and then I found him cheating on me, so I got to keep the ring," she growls.

"Okay, but why didn't you sell it? Get something useful out of it?" I ask.

"Do I look like the kind of girl that needs a man's money?" she snarks with a sassiness I wasn't expecting.

She doesn't need money any more than Siren needs a man's help. But I don't respond. Her question seemed rhetorical, and all I'm doing is digging myself into a deeper hole.

The ring on Nora's finger isn't what has me worried. It's the ring Siren is holding in her hand and looking at like it's poison.

I still, staring at it.

It's a gold ring with dozens of tiny diamonds all around it. It's beautiful, simple, and timeless.

She stares at it. "I thought Hugo worked his ass off to be able to pay for this ring. I thought he scrounged together and saved every last penny to be able to buy me this. I thought it cost thousands. I didn't realize I had the million dollars Hugo owed the drug dealer on my left finger. If I did…"

She would have sold it to free Hugo instead of selling herself to Julian.

I walk over to her. "Is it really worth millions?"

She nods and holds out the ring to me.

I take it and study the intricacy of the ring. There are more diamonds than I first realized.

"It doesn't seem like it should be worth that much."

"A family heirloom. And yes, Hugo's mom told me the value of it last time I visited."

She takes the ring back and slowly puts it on her finger. I hold my breath to keep from making a sound, a twitch, or any movement that would reveal my feelings at seeing another man's ring on her finger.

She takes a deep breath. "Ready."

Siren looks to me and then Nora. We all nod in agreement. Ready. At least as ready as we can be.

We stopped at an expensive clothing store on the way to

the hotel Hugo's parents own, where we will be meeting them and staying. Apparently, jeans were not going to be appropriate attire to meet them in, so I'm wearing khaki slacks and a buttoned-down gray shirt.

Nora is in a flowery dress that seems too sweet for her.

A soft, flowy pink dress hides Siren's curves, the complete opposite of the Siren I know.

"Stop staring at me, stare at Nora. You're supposed to be in love with her, not me," Siren hisses.

"You sure you want to go with pink?"

She sighs. "Yep, it brings out the softness in my eyes."

It does, but the softness in her eyes isn't her best asset.

We all climb into the back of a black town car. Apparently, a taxi wouldn't be appropriate for us to arrive in.

The ride is short, into the heart of Paris. The hotel we stop in front of is the grandest I've ever seen. Suddenly, I think I should have entered in a suit, not khakis. I'm definitely glad I didn't arrive in ripped jeans.

The hotel doorman opens our car door, and Siren walks out like she belongs here. Her face and posture change completely.

I step out, looking completely lost. My hair is up in a bun, my beard is trimmed, and my clothes are tidy, but I'm as far away from belonging here as possible. You can't cover my tattoos or scars, and I sure as hell wasn't letting Siren cut my hair to help me fit in.

"Hold my hand," Nora whispers, her fingers dancing against my palm.

Reluctantly, I take her hand.

"And don't act like it's killing you to be my fiancé. You didn't have such a hard job pretending I was your girlfriend in that bar."

"That's because it was one night, and I was trying to make Siren jealous."

"Well, pretend you're trying to make her jealous again. It worked that night. It can work again."

I lead Nora inside, following Siren. Siren barely waits for us to enter before she's wrapping an extravagantly dressed older woman and a suited, graying haired man in a hug and quick kiss on the cheek.

Yep, should have gone with the suit.

"Aria, it's so good of you to visit," the older woman says.

"It's been too long, but my best friend is getting married, and she wanted the best wedding. So I thought this was just the place and the people to help her get ready for her big day."

"Of course, we are the best," the woman says, looking past Siren to us. A frown immediately appears on her face. Apparently, she doesn't approve of Nora, nor me.

"Let me introduce you to the happy couple," Siren says, ignoring the woman's glare.

"Mrs. Bisset, this is my best friend, Nora Taylor," Siren says.

Mrs. Bisset, who apparently didn't take her husband's last name, holds out a snooty hand to Nora.

"Mrs. Bisset, it's so nice to meet you," Nora says.

The woman just nods as they shake, not offering for Nora to call her by her first name. But then Mrs. Bisset spots Nora's engagement ring.

"Well done, that is an exquisite diamond," Mrs. Bisset says.

Nora nods hesitantly but then grabs my arm. "I snagged a good husband to be."

From the way Mrs. Bisset is looking at me, the only thing

she approves of is the expensive ring I supposedly bought my fiancé. She stares down her nose at me, doubting I could afford it. She doesn't realize if I was getting married for real, I could afford a ring three times as expensive.

"Zeke Kane," I say, introducing myself and not holding out my hand, because I know the woman doesn't want to shake it anyway.

"Hmm," she says.

Siren gives me a quick roll of the eyes only I see.

"And this is Mr. Martinez, he owns a string of hotels here," Siren says.

The man looks up from the phone he has been busy typing on. He nods in our direction, apparently not caring who the new guests are.

"The courtyard out back is the ultimate dream location to get married. The flowers are blooming and beautiful this time of year, but of course, I'll have more flowers brought in for your special day. However, the location and my services do come with a hefty price tag," Mrs. Bisset says, looking at me like I couldn't afford to get married in a barn, much less in a swanky hotel in Paris.

I stare around like this place is nothing more than a Marriot. "It's not up to my tastes, but if my baby here wants it, then I guess this place will do."

Nora smiles, annoyingly, and leans into my chest. I stiffen at how wrong it feels to have any woman leaning against me that isn't Siren.

I'm beginning to think we should have stolen the money from anyone else on the planet. Once we get the money, it's going to feel incredible, but I'm not sure it's worth playing pretend fiancé to a woman who isn't Siren for an entire weekend with these people.

"Oh, look at the time! Dinner will be served in two hours. You will want to get showered and changed before dinner, I'm sure. You'll want to know how the dining room can be transformed, so of course, you'll want to try it out tonight and see it in all its slender."

I sigh. Apparently, what I'm wearing isn't appropriate for dinner with these people. But if I have two hours to change, then at least I'll have two hours away from them. Two hours with Siren—I can think of plenty of things we can do with that time. *She needs, what, thirty minutes to get ready?*

"Ms. Taylor and Mr. Kane, I reserved a suite for you," Mrs. Bisset says.

She snaps her fingers, and a butler appears with our bags to take us up to our room.

My eyes land on Siren. *What room will she be staying in? Where will I need to sneak off to?*

"And Aria dear, you'll be staying in the princess suite as usual. Now, where is your sweet husband?" Mrs. Bisset says.

I stop dead.

Hugo? He's here?

No way! Last time I saw him, I'd broken his kneecap, and Siren had broken his nose and wrist. He should be in a hospital or with Julian doing his bidding. Not here. Not in France. Not with us.

But then I spot him, rounding the corner.

He has crutches, his wrist is in a splint, and he's wearing more makeup than a stage performer to cover the bruises covering his face. But he's here. In a gray suit, somehow looking more refined than I do, even with the crutches.

"Oh, there you are, dear," Mrs. Bisset says, kissing her son on the cheek. "I'm just so happy you two were both able to come. It's been so long since everyone has seen you together. And now that Aria is here, I'm sure you'll heal from that horrible car accident so much faster."

Siren is glaring at Hugo, while I swear there's fear behind his eyes.

Yea, Mrs. Bisset, Hugo will heal a lot faster with Siren here. That, or she'll break his other wrist.

21

SIREN

Hugo is here.

I knew he would be. Mrs. Bisset told me when I called to make the arrangements, but seeing him in person makes me angrier than I expected. He's the only one who could ruin our plans. He knows we aren't here because Zeke and Nora are getting married.

However, he won't rat us out to his parents. Not unless he wants a broken dick to go with his broken wrist and kneecap.

I see the fear in his eyes, but there's also a need for revenge. He wants to stop whatever mission Julian sent me here on. He doesn't know what my mission is, though, or he would have put a stop to this back on the island.

Instead, he goads me. "Come here and give me a kiss, baby."

I hate being called baby, but I walk over and put on a show for his parents. Parents I can't wait to steal everything from. They stole my life by not paying for their son's debt.

The kiss is chaste, our lips barely touch, but I can feel the jealous glare from Zeke on the back of my head.

This is all an act. Stay cool or this won't work. You're supposed to be in love with Nora, not me.

When I pull back from the kiss, Hugo has a smug expression on his face. He knew exactly what he was doing and enjoyed it thoroughly.

"You kids better go upstairs and get ready. Less than two hours until the ball tonight," Mrs. Bisset says.

"We won't be late. But you don't need to throw a party on our account," I say.

"Of course, I do. The world loves seeing the two of you together. And we have a new couple to celebrate," she answers.

I nod.

Zeke and Nora are pushed into one elevator, while Hugo and I are pushed into another, probably headed to different floors and different ends of the hotel. The butlers take our luggage to be delivered and unpacked in our rooms, escaping via servants hallways.

Hugo and I are left alone on the elevator, headed to our usual room.

"So kind of you to stop by France and see how I'm doing. You haven't been here since I dragged your ass here in our early twenties," he says.

"You know me—just wanted to check on my husband after such a horrible car accident and all."

The elevator doors open on the top floor, and I step out, not waiting for Hugo to stumble along with his crutches.

I walk to the door of our suite. It's always the same suite every time we come—only the best for their precious son.

A waiting butler opens the door for me and then holds it open for Hugo.

"Thank you, Travers." Hugo hands him cash. "Could you give us a moment alone please before you start unpacking?"

"Of course, sir. The hairstylists will be up shortly."

Hugo nods at the exiting butler, and we are alone in the gorgeous suite. The suite has three bedrooms, a dining room, a living room, and a dressing room bigger than most bedrooms for us to get ready in. But even though there are three bedrooms, I won't be able to get away with not sleeping in the same bed as Hugo. The maids work for Mrs. Bisset. They will inform her if we don't share a bed.

Hugo leans his crutches against the wall and hops gingerly toward me. I consider walking further into the suite just to make him have to walk further, but I want whatever he has to say over with.

Surprise takes over as he presses a knife against my stomach and shoves me hard against the wall. He drew some blood, although, the pain doesn't register.

I let him think he has me cornered, but even without his broken leg, I can outmaneuver him. He's not a threat.

"What do you want, Hugo?"

"What are you doing here?"

"Working for Julian, same thing I'm always doing. You have yourself to thank for that. Couldn't use Mommy's money to bail yourself out."

He snarls. "Last time I'll ask—what are you doing?" I feel the knife press deeper into my stomach. Even if I couldn't defend myself, he wouldn't really hurt me. At least not in any visible place, he couldn't explain it to his parents.

"Julian sent us. We have someone we need to woo tonight at the party. Someone with lots of money. Don't worry, we will be gone and out of your life again before the weekend is over."

Slice.

I feel it this time. The knife rips through my stomach, making a decent cut. For a second, I can't breathe; the slash hurts me deep and makes my eyes water. I wasn't prepared for him. But breaking a man's wrist and nose will him seek revenge.

It only takes me a second to recover before I punch him in the nose again, making it bleed.

"Fucking bitch! How the hell am I going to explain this?"

I hold my hand over my stomach. "Don't worry, I'm sure your mother hired the best makeup team. They can cover up the bruising. You can just say your nose started bleeding again."

He shoves me hard this time against my wound, making me lose my breath again.

"I'm warning you, Aria. Don't mess with my parents. Don't mess with me. Or I'll make you wish you were dead."

"There is nothing more you can do to me. I've been through too much."

His eyes turn golden with the evilness I didn't realize Hugo possessed until it was too late.

"I'm going to enjoy sleeping with you tonight, Aria. It's been too long."

He releases me. I take a deep breath as the door to our suite opens. I need to take care of my wound before any of the servants see it.

He pockets his knife, wiping the blood from his nose on the back of his hand.

"Unless you're ready to give me that divorce," he says under his breath, threatening more than a knife ever will.

No way in hell I am.

I duck into the bathroom to change my shirt and dress my wound before I spend the next two hours getting ready for the ball tonight.

I get a text from Zeke.

I open it. *Meet me in my room.*

I text back—*Can't. Two hours of hair and makeup.*

He doesn't respond, and my heart aches to be anywhere but here.

I don't want to spend the night with my ex while the man I love pretends to be engaged to another woman. I don't want to spend time with any of these people. But it's the only way to get back at them for what they did to me years ago. And it's the easiest way to steal a billion dollars.

22

—————

ZEKE

I'm wearing a damn tux.

A tux!

I've never worn a tux in my life. I never thought I was going to either. I've never been anywhere fancy enough to need one. A suit is as far as I've ever gone.

"Stop squirming," Nora says as she applies another layer of lipstick in our hotel suite.

The room is fucking huge—plenty big enough for the two of us to share.

"I'm not squirming," I pull at the bowtie at my neck.

Nora just glares at me in the mirror.

I sigh and stop messing with the tie. My hair is slicked back in a bun. My face is cleanshaven. I have enough cologne on that you can probably smell me coming from a hallway away.

Nora stands in her light blue dress. She seems to shimmer as she walks in the slinky dress.

"You look nice," I say.

She raises an eyebrow. "Just nice? This is Gucci. These are Cartier diamonds. This is better than nice."

I rub my neck. "Fine, you look beautiful. Better?"

She nods. "You look handsome as well."

I stare down at my tux. "Really? I feel like a penguin."

She laughs and loops her arm around my elbow.

I stiffen.

She notices. "You've got it bad, huh?"

"Yes," there is no reason not to tell her the truth.

"You're making Aria jealous, remember? Flirt with me and pretend it's her. Every time she looks at you, it will only make her want you more. Trust me."

I nod. I don't really have a choice. We've chosen Hugo's parents as our target. And they think Siren and Hugo are in a loving marriage. I can't walk in with her on my arm. This is the only way to get close enough to steal the money.

"Let's go. We wouldn't want to be late," Nora says.

"Of course not. We wouldn't want to be late to meeting all of Mrs. Bisset's rich, snooty, stuck up friends."

We head down the elevator and walk through the lobby toward the ballroom, looking very much the couple as Nora keeps her hand in the crook of my elbow and tells me funny stories about Siren to distract me and keep me smiling.

"Names?" a man asks when we reach the ballroom.

"Zeke Kane and soon to be Mrs. Kane," I smile, acting completely ridiculous and out of character as I kiss Nora on the cheek.

Nora smiles back, happy with my act.

The servant is pleased as well, because we're quickly allowed to enter.

"Holy fuck," I curse as I stare wide-eyed at the room.

Nora smirks. "Welcome to the world of the rich and famous." She snags us two champagne flutes off a tray and hands one to me.

"I'm going to need something stronger than this," I say.

She shakes her head. "First champagne, then wine at dinner. The hard stuff doesn't come out until later."

I moan.

"Come on, let's go find our table," Nora says, navigating me through the room like this is where she belongs.

"So I take it this isn't your first time in a room like this?" I ask as we find our seats at a table in the corner of the room.

"Nope, I was brought up in society life like this. But don't act like you don't have money or designer clothes. Just because you prefer a nice pair of jeans over a tux doesn't mean you don't have money."

"I do have money. I just would never spend it on things like this."

And then everyone's attention in the room turns toward a grand staircase at the far side of the room that no one has been on. A man has a microphone and is announcing the arrival of our hosts—Mrs. Bisset and Mr. Martinez.

Mr. Martinez escorts his wife effortlessly down the stairs as everyone cheers and thanks them. It feels like such a ridiculous show.

Then the announcer asks the room to stand and welcome back Mr. and Mrs. Martinez.

I hold my breath and wait as the double doors open, and Siren and Hugo step out.

He isn't using his crutches. Instead, he grips Siren's arm tightly, using her as his crutch, taking baby steps. It makes no sense for them to enter down the stairs. They should be entering through the regular entrance and take the elevator. But nothing about this world makes much sense to me.

Not the gold plated dinnerware, the real silver silverware, the crystal glasses, or the chandelier that's bigger than a car. Nor the thousands of dollars worth of flowers that are only going to be used a single night.

But when I turn my attention to Siren, finally taking her in, everything about this world suddenly makes sense. Siren is wearing a rose gold gown. A gown that hugs every curve. She shines brighter than anything in this room. The dress is sexy as hell—it has a long train on the back, and she wears heels that make her six feet tall.

Her makeup intensifies every feature on her face—her catlike eyes, plump lips, and pink cheeks. Her hair is curled and pinned up on her head, with only a few strands hanging down.

Siren is why a room like this exists. Without it, Siren would never wear a dress like that, and that would be a shame. She was born to be dressed in beautiful clothes and jewels.

Siren is beautiful in jeans and no makeup. She's beautiful in rags, but this version of Siren demands everyone's attention. No one speaks like they did for Hugo's parents. Everyone just stares, showing their appreciation for the couple with their silence.

Finally, the couple makes it down the stairs to Hugo's parents. Mrs. Bisset starts speaking into a microphone, welcoming everyone, introducing her son and beautiful daughter-in-law, and gushing about how excited she is to host a party in their honor.

It's clear she threw this ball not so Nora and I could see her event planning skills and what she could do for our fake wedding, but because she wants to show off her son and daughter-in-law.

Mrs. Bisset ends her speech, and everyone begins to scatter. I lose sight of Siren.

I stand, intending to go find her, when Nora touches my arm, telling me to stay.

I realize then that everyone is taking their seats to eat.

The dinner lasts two hours. A dinner where I had to listen to a lawyer talk about divorce settlements, and a wine connoisseur talk about how a different wine would have been better with the duck.

"These people are so boring," I say to Nora.

She chuckles. "Why do you think I learned to fly? So I could leave whenever I wanted."

I clink my wine glass with hers and drink to that.

Finally, our dessert plates are removed, and the dancing portion of the night starts. I swear this night is right out of the 1920s. I didn't know people still behaved like this.

"Dance with me," I say to Nora.

She smiles. "You only want to get closer to Siren."

I shrug. "We can also be in search of finding you a man for the night."

"How scandalous." Nora puts her hand over her mouth and fakes outrage.

I roll my eyes but smile as I lead her to the dance floor.

Hugo may have been able to hobble down the stairs and hide his injuries, but there is no way he can dance. This is my chance to get closer to Siren.

I lead Nora onto the dance floor even though I don't know how to dance to this classical music.

Nora laughs. "I'll lead."

She does a fine job, and I'm a fast learner, so we glide across the floor.

As expected, I don't see Siren on the dance floor. But after a few minutes, I do feel her gaze on the back of my head.

It lights my eyes up.

Nora, of course, notices as the song ends. "Go get our girl. Now's your chance. I need a moment to freshen up in the bathroom anyway."

I give her a little bow I've seen the other men do like she's a princess or something.

"Not bad, you're catching on. A few more hours in this world, and you'd be a pro."

"Nope, I'd have to chop off the hair. And that's not happening."

She laughs and then leaves the dance floor. I head in the direction of the intense feeling I have behind me, knowing it's Siren.

But I'm too focused on her that I don't see him.

"Zeke, a word," Hugo says in a crowd of people, ensuring I can't say no without making a scene. I nod angrily and follow Hugo away from the ballroom and out into a small balcony.

"Stay away from Aria," Hugo says.

So that's why he's so pissy.

I fold my arms looking bored. "No."

"It wasn't a request. You are in my world. Aria will be sleeping in my bed tonight. Do as I say, or she'll pay the consequences."

I notice he's wearing even more makeup than before, but it does nothing to hide the new bruising around his eye.

I smile. "Looks like Siren can take care of herself just fine."

He growls, but then it turns dangerous. "And I can take care of myself."

His words stun me. *What did he do?* I didn't see any physical mark on Siren, but if he raped her, I wouldn't see anything.

I grab the asshole by the neck and push him until he's dangling over the edge of the railing.

He grabs onto my wrist. "Don't threaten Siren. I swear if you touched her—"

"You'll what? You're up to something. Something Julian ordered. If you fail, he'll kill your friend—Lucy, was it?"

Fuck, I still haven't had time to move her and make sure she's safe.

I pull him back just a little.

"If I find out you touched her, or if you hurt her in any way, I'll kill you. That's a promise." And then I punch him hard in the gut and pull him back over the balcony.

I head back inside the ballroom just in time to see a ghost.

Kai Miller.

My boss, Enzo's Black's girl. The last person I wanted to see here. She stands taller than the last time I saw her. Her hair is twisted up, similar to Siren's. She demands attention and respect. I look around for Enzo but don't find him anywhere. *Why would she be here? And without him?*

He's here. He wouldn't let her out of his sight. *Unless...*

Nope, not going there.

Kai's eyes seem sad. But then her eyes cut to me. They land on me for less than a second. But in that second, I see everything—surprise, concern, hope. And then her face returns to vagueness, like she's unfazed by seeing me here.

She got my note.

I see the black scrunchie around her arm—a scrunchie I gave to her just before I was shot and lost to the sea.

I smile.

For a second, I wonder if I should run to Kai and go find Enzo with her. My heart hurts at seeing one of my closest friends again and not being able to hug her.

Our worlds will cross again. But tonight isn't that night. I'm here on a mission, not to reminisce with old friends. I'm doing this to prevent them from having one more enemy when I get back.

Just a little longer. Make sure Lucy is safe. Finish this job, learn about Julian's bank accounts, and then leave. If I can liquidate Julian's bank accounts until he has nothing, then he won't be able to come after me. Siren will have no money to chase me with. No army. I would have protected my friends.

23

KAI

WATCHING one of my best friends die shook me to my very core, but finding his note in our vault telling me he was alive was one of the happiest moments of my life. Every day since, I've wanted to find him. I've wanted to chase after him. Hunt him down and bring him home to Enzo and me.

But I had to trust that Zeke had a good reason to not return to the living. That he needed to remain dead to those who loved him.

I honored that. *Really, I did.*

It was just coincidence that we are both in the same ballroom in Paris. I'm here to meet a man who has new technology to improve the security system on our yachts. It's an easy meeting, and Enzo decided to stay back with the kids instead of mingling with snooty, rich snobs. *He got the better job.*

Until I saw Zeke.

My heart stopped when I saw him in the flesh.

I knew he was alive all this time.

But seeing him, my heart lept. It came alive in a way it

hasn't since falling in love with the man of my dreams and getting my own happily ever after.

I wanted to run to Zeke. I wanted to hug him and drag him home with me. Tell him whatever trouble he is in, whatever enemies he's made, we don't care. We are a family, and we fight our battles together.

But when I looked into Zeke's eyes, I knew today isn't the day to bring him home. That he still has battles he needs to face, alone.

I still don't understand why. And it's taking everything in me not to send my men after him.

But then I see her. The most beautiful woman is staring at me with complete fascination. As she looks from me and then searches for Zeke in the crowd, I make the connection. I know who this woman is. I may not know her name. I may not know her life story. But I know who she is. She's the reason Zeke hasn't come home.

He's in love with her.

She could be his happily ever after.

Or she could break his heart.

He needs more time. I'll give it to him, even though it kills me to keep his secret. To know he's alive while everyone else mourns his death.

Only a little longer, Zeke. I can't wait forever for you to come home.

24

SIREN

THIS ENTIRE NIGHT has been horrible. I hate having to talk to rich people who don't give a shit about me. They just want to judge what I'm wearing and the fact that I haven't visited my in-laws in years.

If they only knew the truth, that I was here to steal a billion dollars from them, then they'd really have something to judge.

I spot Hugo and Zeke head out on the balcony to talk or fight; I'm not sure. I want to go with them, but I know Zeke doesn't need me to fight his battles. He can handle Hugo just fine. And this gives me a chance to enact the plan without Hugo noticing.

I need to find Mr. Martinez. The goal is simple. Steal his phone and hope it has the security information we need to hack their bank account. I'm a bit rusty when it comes to hacking, but Zeke says he has the skills if we can get the phone. Or that he knows someone he can contact to hack it if he can't handle it.

So tonight's job is simple. Get the damn phone from Mr. Martinez. Should be easy enough since he always has his phone on him. But he's always surrounded by people, and he's not exactly my biggest fan, so getting close to him has been difficult without Mrs. Bisset stepping in and wanting to introduce me to another couple.

I spot Mr. Martinez ordering a whiskey from the bar.

Now's my chance. I make my way through the crowd of people toward him, but something odd catches my attention as I walk—a woman wearing a black scrunchie around her wrist.

Very odd for such a formal night.

I can't stop looking at her. I take in everything about her —dark hair, olive skin, sparkly skin-hugging dress, high heels, diamonds, and a black scrunchie on her wrist.

A scrunchie completely out of place. I can't take my eyes off the scrunchie. I have this weird feeling I've seen it before. A sense of déjà vu washes over me; I'm suspended in time.

Who is this woman?

Finally, I let my eyes drift up. She's deep in a conversation with two men, completely controlling them with her words and body language. She's here on business.

But she must feel me staring because she turns her head in my direction. Our exchange of glances is the most bizarre thing I've ever felt, and yet, it's the most peaceful.

She gives me a tight-lipped smile, nodding at me as if she knows a secret I don't and approves.

I look at her in confusion, which makes her smile kindly at me.

Then all at once, it hits me who she is. She's from Zeke's world before. She thought he was dead, which is why she carries the scrunchie with her everywhere.

My heart breaks for her and for me. It's clear she loves Zeke as much as I do. *Has Zeke seen her? Does he know she's here?*

The woman shakes her head, as if to say, 'No, don't tell him.'

Apparently, she's a mind reader too.

I frown. This woman is beautiful and strong. She's probably not a liar like me. She's probably always told Zeke the truth.

How many women in Zeke's life do I have to compete with? Lucy? This woman? How many more?

Zeke is easy to fall in love with, so it wouldn't surprise me if he had hoards of women in love with him.

I see Mr. Martinez moving out of the corner of my eye toward the stairs. He's leaving for the night.

This is my last chance. I have to go now. But I want to ask this woman so many questions. I want to know how to protect Zeke. I want to know how to return him to the world he belongs in.

Choose now.

Stick to the plan.

So instead of questioning the woman who holds all the answers to Zeke, I head after Mr. Martinez.

There isn't much time for a plan on how to get the phone, so I do the only thing I can think of. I bump into him. I retrieve the phone easily from his pocket and hold it begin my back.

"I'm so sorry, Mr. Martinez," I say.

He huffs and then continues up the stairs.

When I turn back, the woman I saw before was gone. It was almost like I'd seen a ghost.

I turn toward the balcony and see Hugo and Zeke re-entering the ballroom.

Both men spot me.

I sigh. And then plaster a fake smile on my face as I make my way over to them.

I nod at Zeke as I pass him, slipping the phone into his jacket pocket. But that's all the interaction I give him. He needs to go find Nora and spend the night hacking into the phone and bank account.

"Ready to leave?" I ask Hugo.

He holds his hand against his stomach like he's in pain.

I grin. *What did Zeke do to you?*

He slips his hand around my arm, using me like a crutch. We walk slowly to the elevator. I consider calling for a wheelchair, but I know he wouldn't allow it. So instead of a five-minute walk to the suite, it takes us twenty.

Finally, we get to the door, I unlock it, and once Hugo is inside, I release his hold on me. I don't care if he never makes it to the bedroom.

I walk straight to the dressing room to remove my dress and caked-on makeup. I spend a long time scrubbing my face clean. I put on pajama pants and T-shirt before heading to bed. Somehow, Hugo has found his way to the bed and is rolled over on his side, facing away from me. And from what I can tell, he's shirtless.

Please let him be wearing pants.

I walk around to the far side of the bed and pull the covers back that have already been turned down by the maids.

I can't tell what Hugo is wearing, but I see the waistband of something, so he isn't naked.

"Touch me, and I'll kill you," I say, pulling the covers up.

Hugo doesn't respond. Maybe he's asleep.

I close my eyes and immediately feel the pull of sleep. Tonight exhausted me. I need to shut my brain off. I can't think about Hugo, or stealing Mr. Martinez's phone, or the woman with the scrunchie, or Zeke. I just need to shut the world out and decompress for a few hours; then I can face the world tomorrow.

Sleep pulls me hard. When I drink too much, like tonight, sleep comes easily and hard.

Sleep.

He's here. He came for me—Zeke.

I feel his presence. I feel him pressed up against me, his erection at my ass begging for entrance.

I smile and lift my legs to allow him better access.

He pushes his cock between my legs but doesn't enter me yet.

I feel his rough hands at my breasts. *Yes, tease me.*

His hands are rougher than I remember. He's not gentle, but then he never really is. But this is different—frantic, almost angry.

Something's not right.

Stop.

Wake up.

Tell him to stop.

"Stop," I whisper.

But he doesn't stop touching me, pushing himself on me.

I start fighting back, but my eyes are too heavy to open. *Wake up! Don't let this happen!*

I fight harder.

My tears are stinging my eyes.

"Stop," I say louder.

He doesn't listen. Zeke always listens. This isn't Zeke. The man hurting me is someone much worse...

Hugo.

His name on my tongue wakes me up, jolting me awake.

He's on top of me, using the pull of sleep to try and have his way with me.

Fucking bastard.

My arms are pinned, tied together, and pushed over my head. My shirt is pushed up; my pants are ripped and barely hang onto my waist.

"Stop," I say calmly, hoping my calm will end this frenzy. It doesn't.

"Hugo," I say, and my voice catches his attention. He looks at me, past the anger, and really looks at me.

"Stop, please. This isn't you. You aren't this person."

He shakes his head. "You don't know who I am or what I've become. Not anymore."

"Yes, I do. I fell in love with you. I know the depths of your heart. I could even love you again. But I won't if you do this. There is no way to ask forgiveness for this. If you do this, there is no going back."

He pauses as if deciding, but I don't trust Hugo to make the right decision. I've been manipulating him this whole time, distracting him until I could get my hands free. And finally, I did. I'm not going to wait to see if he has a heart. I protect myself at all costs.

I snap his neck, immediately putting him into a deep sleep. He won't wake up for several hours.

I pant heavily, and then I push him off me onto the other side of the bed.

I need air. I can't breathe.

I get up from the bed, realizing how close I came to being raped. If he was better at tying my hands or if he had managed to tie up my legs before I woke up, I wouldn't have been able to protect myself. He would have raped me. He could have killed me if he wanted.

I head to the bathroom and splash some water on my face. And then I stare at myself in the mirror.

That was close. Too close. I'm better than this. I don't let anyone get close. I don't let myself be vulnerable. I protect myself. I save myself. Because no other man will.

Zeke—his name floats into my head. Zeke would have saved me.

I shake my head. He would have wanted to. But he wasn't here. He didn't save me. I saved myself. I can't rely on Zeke. I can't rely on any man. I'm my only protector. And I almost failed.

25

ZEKE

Nora wanted me to stay in our hotel room all night and work on breaking into the phone. But I was able to break into the phone within five minutes. The phone had a simple password, and his bank account was accessible right on the app.

Siren was right, Hugo's parents are loaded. We can steal the billion dollars from them. We have everything we need.

Tomorrow, we can leave. But tonight, we are stuck here.

"Just sleep, Zeke. Time will go by faster if you sleep. Tomorrow we have a long day of flying back. Sleep, you'll see Siren tomorrow," Nora says before yawning.

"I can't sleep. Not with that fucker sleeping in the bed next to her."

"They won't share a bed. Their suite is bigger than ours."

I raise an eyebrow. "They will share a bed, or the maids will know they are fighting."

"Oh."

"Yea...oh."

Suddenly, I get the strangest feeling. A feeling that disturbs me to the bones.

"Something isn't right," I say, running my hand through my hair as I grab the room key.

"Where are you going?" Nora asks, jumping up like her tiny frame is going to stop me.

"I need to make sure Siren is alright."

"Zeke, you can't. She's fine. She's a big girl. She can protect herself. Just try to sleep or watch TV or something. We can check on her in the morning."

I look at Nora. She doesn't get it, but Siren and I share a connection I don't understand. I can feel when she's in pain or happy. I just know when she's experiencing the worst emotions.

"This can't wait until morning. She's in trouble," I say.

"Zeke..." Nora starts again.

I open the door and stop.

"Be careful, please. And let me know when you find her, and she's alright. Or I'll worry."

I smile. "Will do."

I don't know which room Siren and Hugo are staying in. I just know the room is the best.

So I head to the elevator bank and hit the top floor, hoping that when I get there, it will be obvious which room is theirs. If not, I'll be sneaking into a lot of suites until I find the right one. Nothing is stopping me right now; something is wrong. And if Hugo touched her, I'm going to kill him.

The elevator doors open to the top floor, and there are almost as many rooms up here as there are on my floor. That is until you walk to the far corner. There is only one door for most of this corridor. It's by far the biggest room in the hotel.

This is their room.

I lean my ear against the door, trying to hear if they are awake, but it's silent. They have top-level security here, so if

I don't seem like I belong, a guard will be here in minutes to escort me away.

I lift my card to the door for the cameras, as I slip the small screwdriver below the keycard to unlock the door. But the cameras only see me flash my keycard, and the light turns green.

I carefully step inside, putting the tool and card back into my pocket as I step into the darkness. From what I can make out, the suite seems a few rooms bigger than mine but is otherwise decorated the same. With gold and art, and a lot of breakable shit.

I head through the living quarters toward the bedrooms. I poke my head in the first two, but as I knew, Siren isn't in either. That leaves the master bedroom, where they both are.

The door is cracked, but not closed.

I stand next to it, listening carefully, but I only hear the gentle sound of them breathing.

Hmm. That's weird? I thought for sure something was wrong.

Slowly, I open the door, thankful the door doesn't creak, and then I walk into the dark room.

Hugo is sleeping on one side, and Siren is sleeping on the other.

I walk over to her side to study her closer and make sure she's okay. She seems to be sleeping deeply, her breathing deep and heavy.

I pull out my phone and text Nora that Siren is fine, asleep in her bed.

I should leave her to sleep. I should head back, but I can't stand being so close to Siren and not having her. Not tasting her. Not making definitively sure she's okay.

So I lean down, and then I put my hand over her mouth to keep her from screaming and waking Hugo up.

She immediately bucks and punches me hard in the nose, fighting for her life, not realizing it's me.

Yea, I made a mistake with the hand over the mouth move.

"Siren, it's me, Zeke," I whisper.

But she keeps trying to fight me, even as I pull her out of the bed and carry her to the bathroom. I lock the door and turn on the lights so she can see me.

Her eyes open when the lights flicker on, and I remove my hand from her mouth and step back.

"It's me," I say again.

She takes a second to catch her breath, her eyes blinking, assuring herself that I'm standing here in her bathroom, and this isn't a dream.

Then she runs to me and collapses against my chest, her arms wrapping around my waist tightly.

I grab her, holding me hard against me.

I was right. Something is clearly wrong.

But I don't ask her about it. If she wants to talk, she will, when she's ready.

"How did you know to come?" she finally asks.

"I don't know. I just knew something was wrong."

She nods into my chest.

And then her hands are working their way up my body to my chest, then neck. She pulls me down, and my head dips to meet her for a perfect kiss.

A kiss that tells me everything I need to know. She's scared. Me being here is everything. *Thank you. Don't ever leave.*

I push my tongue into her mouth, fisting her hair, keeping her lips against mine. They say my reply for me. *I'm here. I'm not leaving.*

I want to add—*ever*. But that's a promise I can't keep. A promise I shouldn't want to keep.

I grab her ass and lift her up until she's sitting on the vanity. We need a different kind of connection right now.

"God, I love fucking you everywhere, but someday I'd really like to fuck you in a bed again. Nothing beats a bed."

She laughs nervously. "Agreed."

Nervous? Why?

I step between her spread legs studying her for a second, but she just pulls my face back to hers to kiss me harder, not wanting me to see her anxiety.

So I ignore it for now. Fucking her is the best medicine to reduce the nerves she's feeling at whatever Hugo threatened her with.

I put everything I have into the kiss. On her lips, her neck, the perfect spot at the base of her neck before her skin disappears in her shirt.

But I'm greedy. I want all of her.

I grab her shirt and lift it up over her head before I take her nipple in my mouth.

She stiffens.

I stop.

What's wrong? Did I bite down too roughly? What's going on?

And then I see it.

The bandage over her stomach.

Siren tries to push my hands away, but I have to know. I need to know what happened to her.

I put my hand on the bandage, wishing my hands alone would be enough to take away her pain. I look into her eyes, desperate to see what's beneath the bandage, but I won't remove it without her permission.

She sucks in a breath for just a second and then nods.

Carefully, I peel back the bandage, keeping my eyes on

her. Trying to reassure her that whatever lies beneath, I will get revenge for. I will find a way to fix it.

When I see the gash on her smooth stomach, my heart hardens. I'm pissed. Beyond pissed. All I see is red. I want to murder whoever did this, and I don't have to ask who.

But this wound isn't fresh. This happened earlier. This is what Hugo was referring to on the balcony.

"What else?" I ask, my voice softer than I feel. I need to know what else Hugo did. *What had her so scared tonight?* Because this injury didn't cause her fear. She fought back and hurt Hugo as badly as he hurt her. A gash on the stomach, while looking bad, is only skin deep. He didn't really hurt her. I'm not even sure it will scar long term.

But he did something. Said something. Did something that scared her in a way this didn't.

"Truth or si—" I start, hoping the game we play will convince her to talk. Or at least give her a way out if she doesn't want to talk where I can't get angry with her.

But she presses her fingers to my lips, silencing me.

She bites her lip, then opens her mouth. "I want both. To talk and to sin. Don't make me choose."

"You can have both."

She nods. "When I was asleep..." her voice catches, and she takes a deep breath before starting again. "When I was asleep, Hugo tried to rape me."

Her words hurt worse than a bullet to the heart. The snake tried to hurt her. *Tried, she said tried, right?* I'm not just hoping that he didn't do more than attempt.

I wait. She has more to say.

"I woke up, and he had my arms tied up. He was on top of me, ripping my clothes off."

I stare down at her pants for the first time, realizing her pants are ripped.

"Fuck," I exhale, needing to get rid of some of my anger before I explode.

"I was able to keep him talking until my hands got free."

Thank god.

"And then I snapped his neck."

I look at the door. *The bastard deserved worse.*

"He's not dead; he's just passed out."

I nod. But he won't live for much longer.

Siren grabs my cheeks and turns my face back to her. Hesitantly, she leans down until our lips are close, but not touching. Her eyes are watery. Her hands tremble. Her throat is tight.

But she takes a deep breath over my lips, and I know I'm easing her pain. Just being with me does that to her. Just like it's easing my anger.

"Make me forget, Zeke. Make me yours."

There is an unspoken sentence she's not saying—make love to me Zeke. She's not asking me to fuck her. She's asking for gentle, for slow. For something that feels like love and not lust. She wants to be taken care of. The only thing I could possibly want more at the moment is to destroy the man who made her feel this vulnerable.

I hear a man stirring outside the bathroom door. But Siren doesn't. She's focused on me.

I can kill two birds with one stone. I can make love to her, and let Hugo know he will never touch her again. That his time is limited. That Siren is mine, not his.

I had hoped to fuck her quietly in the bathroom, but now, I'm going to make sure Hugo and every other person in this hotel know exactly who Siren belongs to—me.

I kneel down in front of her, kissing over her stomach wound. Her eyes light up—big, gorgeous dark eyes that reveal how good my lips feel on her stomach.

I hook my fingers around the waistband of her pants and slowly bring them down, keeping an eye on her the whole time and letting her feel in control. In control enough to keep any memories of what Hugo tried to do out of her memory.

Carefully, I spread her legs as I kiss every spot of skin from her toes to her thighs, taking my time as I worship her body with my mouth.

She grips the edge of the counter, lets her head fall back, but keeps her eyes locked on me. I can't break eye contact with her. She needs to know it's me doing the wonderful things to her body.

This is as intimate as it gets. She's trusting me with her pain, her heart. I make love to her without falling myself.

I can do this. I can make love without being in love.

A soft, throaty cry escapes her lips. It's beautiful and painful and tells me everything she's not saying. *Stop the pain, ease the pain. You're the only man who can.*

Dammit—if that doesn't make me fall a little, nothing will.

"I got you," I say, gently opening her legs for my mouth to find her delicious pussy. I'm slower than I've ever been with her. Taking my time as I tenderly kiss over her. Not yet using my tongue, just lighting up every nerve and bringing all the blood south, so her head doesn't have to think anymore.

I want Siren to come.

I want her to explode on my lips, on my hand, on my cock. As I finally let my tongue out to flick over her clit, I realize the main difference between fucking and making love, and it's not how fast you go. The difference is sex is about mutual pleasure. It's about chasing your own orgasm as well as hers. Making love is selfless. It's putting her needs above my own until her needs are all that matter. Siren is all that matters.

Looking at her now, naked and spread for me, sharing a vulnerable secret to show me she isn't always strong. She was inches away from failing to protect herself. She isn't a seductive manipulative monster like I thought. She's a woman doing her best to survive in very much a man's world.

Every man in this world is a danger to her. Every man is bigger. Stronger. More powerful.

And every man in the underworld is capable of rape and murder.

Siren is always vulnerable.

But not anymore.

Because whether she likes it or not, I'm here to protect her.

I lick her slow, finding every button to push between her legs. Exploring her like I've never explored her before. Always keeping my eyes on her. Watching to ensure she's enjoying every second.

I see it the moment she's mine completely. Her eyes widen, she bites down on her lip to hold in her moan, and she grips the counter like she's holding onto a bucking horse.

I put my hand over hers, squeezing gently, reminding her I'm in this with her. That I'm not letting go.

Her teeth rake over her bottom lip as her body tries to contain her impending orgasm, but I've built her so slowly for so long that the explosion is going to greater than any we've experienced.

"Zeke! Yes, fuck Zeke! Yes!" she screams as my tongue dips inside her just in time to feel her contracting around me, her sweet taste filling my mouth. A taste I can never get enough of.

I give her a minute to come down from her high. I continue to kneel in front of her, watching her, worshipping her.

Finally, she touches my face as her cheeks flush. "More." Her eyes light up with what she wants to do next.

Thank fuck, because I'm going to die if I don't get to fuck her soon.

SIREN

Zeke found me. He would have been too late to protect me from Hugo if Hugo had succeeded in raping me, but he would have been here to comfort me and kill Hugo for what he did.

I don't care about any of that. I care about Zeke kneeling in front of me like he would give me the world if I asked.

Zeke came to find me without even changing out of the tuxedo he hates but looking hot as fuck in. The pants show off the curve of his ass, and the jacket bulges around his biggest muscles—his arms and chest. There is just something about a bad boy with tattoos and a man bun all dressed up in something refined that just does something to me.

But what has my toes curling and my heart thumping the most is the way he took care of me. The way he put my needs above his own and made me come in a way he never has before.

He did what I wanted even though I couldn't speak the words—*he made love to me.*

I need *more*. I want the delicious stretch as he enters me.

I want his thick muscles flexing over me as he drives inside me. I want to see the soft expression on his face turn carnal as he loses control.

Zeke is still kneeling in front of me, so I lean forward and brush my hands inside his jacket, pushing it off his shoulders. He lets it fall to the floor.

Then I grab his bowtie, tugging it up until he's standing in front of me.

For the last fifteen minutes, Zeke has kept eye contact with me. He's looked into my soul, knowing I needed the deepest connection with him to keep from breaking. To keep from reliving how close I was to being violated.

But my goal now is to make his eyes roll back from pleasure, just not yet.

I undo his bowtie slowly, every movement feeling as much like a tease as our lips brushing together.

The bowtie falls to the floor. I begin undoing every shirt button slowly.

"You're killing me," he says so softly. So kindly. The gentle giant. The man capable of so much pain showing kindness.

My eyes flutter. This isn't what lust feels like. This is what love feels like. But I don't say it. I can't. Because if I tell him I love him, and he doesn't say it back, I will die. Everything I've done for months now will have been for nothing. These last seven years would be for nothing, because fate put in this position—to save Zeke.

Saving Zeke matters more than just saving him for myself. Zeke is meant for greatness. Only he can save more. Save the masses. While I can only save him.

Slowly, Zeke removes his shirt while I unbutton and unzip his pants.

He doesn't wait for me this time. His pants and boxer briefs fall to the floor, and we are both naked.

I suck in a breath. Zeke is standing between my legs, our eyes still together. He doesn't drive into me immediately. He holds my head and locks our lips while maintaining eye contact.

He lets my hands explore his muscular body, getting reacquainted with him. He lifts me from the counter and turns us to the door. At first, I don't know why, and then I hear him—Hugo.

He's ensuring Hugo can't get to me by fucking me against the door. He's letting Hugo hear what Zeke gets that he doesn't.

It turns me on to see how much Zeke needs Hugo to know that I'm Zeke's, no one else's.

"This okay?" he asks, his cock resting at my entrance as he holds me, my back against the door.

I can barely hear Hugo anymore, but I want him to hear everything. I want him to hear what it sounds like when I'm fucked by a real man. By a man I want. A man I love.

This is what Hugo could have had if he had loved me back. If he hadn't betrayed me. If he never tried to hurt me.

"Fuck me, Zeke."

His cock is inside me in one slow stroke.

I suck in a breath.

"No, this isn't fucking. This is more," he says. His forehead rests against mine, our eyes as close as possible without going cross.

He moves inside me. "So much more."

Zeke takes his time thrusting inside me. My slick walls are welcoming him in hungrily. My body is already coming alive for a second time around him.

I kiss him, pushing my tongue and pulling for everything he can give me as my fingers claw at his back.

And he gives me everything. Every thrust. Grunt. Moan. Every scream he has.

He hits each spot he should and somehow finds new spots inside me to turn on and drive me wild.

"Siren! Jesus, I'm close, Siren!"

I tangle my hand in his hair. "Zeke! Yes, Zeke!"

We come, slamming hard against the wall, until it's undeniable what we are doing—fucking each other's brains out.

Zeke continues to thrust, making sure he pulls every drop of my orgasm from me, but he never loses eye contact with me. I'm his world right now.

"Zeke, I lo—oh, fuck!" I say, my feelings almost slipping out.

Zeke just kisses me. I don't know if he realizes what I was about to say, or he just wanted to kiss me.

I hear the angry pounding on the other side of the door.

"I think we might have woken him up. Oops," Zeke says, but he isn't sorry at all.

He stares at the tub. "We should soak, but I don't want you anywhere near Hugo for a moment longer than you need to be," he says.

"We can take a bath in your room. I'm not staying here. Not a moment longer."

He nods. "I don't think we should stay in this hotel tonight. Not after..."

I frown. I'm not sure what he means. Yes, we fucked, and Hugo knows about it, but I doubt he will tell anyone. Unless he thinks one of the night guards heard us, which is definitely possible.

"Okay. Then we will drive or catch a train out of here and fly out on the first flight tomorrow."

He nods.

We both reluctantly get dressed. Neither of us wants to leave this room. Out there, we have to face the world. In here, we only have to face each other.

Once we are both dressed, Zeke asks, "Ready?"

I nod.

Zeke takes my hand and keeps me behind his body, shielding me from whatever we will face on the other side of the door. He switches the lock, grabs the handle and turns, pushing the door open.

Hugo is sitting on the edge of the bed, waiting for us.

As soon as we emerge, he springs up and tries to grab me, but Zeke only moves in front of me more, pushing me further back, shielding me.

"Aria is my wife! She's not your plaything. She's my wife!" Hugo yells.

"No! She's not your damn wife! Maybe on paper, but only because you set some trap in the prenup she signed. But in every other sense, she's mine!" Zeke yells.

She's mine.

I shiver, his words washing through me until they warm my soul. *I'm his. He's mine.*

But for how much longer? The doubt immediately creeps in.

Zeke lets go of my hand, and the looming danger raises the hair on my arms.

I reach for my gun but realize I'm an idiot; I didn't sleep with a gun. I was worried Hugo would grab it while I was sleeping and use it on me. Probably smart since he was able to pin me down in my sleep. *If he had had a gun, what would he have done to me?*

I'm defenseless expect for my fists and wit, standing in my pajamas. Zeke, though, isn't defenseless. He has his gun out and aimed at Hugo within seconds.

I knew I felt danger, but it thought it was an outside source coming in. I didn't realize the danger was coming from Zeke.

"Zeke, what are you doing?" I ask, trying to keep my voice calm.

Zeke ignores me. He looks at Hugo, who has his hands up and fear in his eyes as he takes a step back. Hugo is no match for Zeke. Hugo is just a dumb man who got lost in a world he didn't belong in. Sure, he can fight, but not like Zeke. Hugo isn't ignorant enough to think the security in this hotel would be able to protect him.

"You hurt Siren. You slashed her stomach. You tried to take from her without her permission. Do you remember what I said I would do if you hurt Siren?"

"You said you would kill me," Hugo answers his voice dry.

Zeke nods. "I'm a man of my word."

"No!" I scream, dashing in front of Hugo to protect him.

Zeke blinks rapidly, not expecting me to save this disgusting man again. And shocked from the fact that he almost shot me, instead of Hugo.

"Siren, move," Zeke says.

"No, you can't kill Hugo," I answer. *There is so much you don't know, Zeke. Just trust me. This is what saving me looks like —not getting revenge.*

Zeke's eyes don't leave mine. He will do what I ask even though it pisses him off to not kill Hugo.

Zeke drops his gun wordlessly and walks to the door.

I glare at Hugo.

"Thank you," Hugo says, realizing Zeke really meant to kill him.

"I didn't save you for you."

"I know."

I follow Zeke out the door and back to his room for a brief second to throw his things in a bag and give me time to change out of pajamas and into Nora's clothes. I didn't bother to pack up my own.

Zeke doesn't talk to me the entire time. Nora notices but doesn't ask what's going on between us. She also doesn't ask why we are packing up in the middle of the night.

We got what we came here for—the phone. Hopefully, it's enough to hack into their bank accounts to steal the money.

I look at Zeke, who will no longer meet my eyes. It's going to take a long time for him to be warm to me again, if he ever does. In Zeke's eyes, I chose Hugo over him. I didn't.

I was choosing myself. Protecting myself. And if there was a way I could have chosen Zeke, I would have. But he wasn't even an option. He will never be an option.

We ride a train and then a plane. This time I sit with Nora. There won't be any sneaking off to go fuck in the bathroom on this flight—not this time.

When Zeke finally starts snoring in his chair across the aisle, I bury my head in Nora's chest and let the tears fall. I got what I wanted. I got Zeke to claim me as his. I got one lovemaking session. Then it was all taken away a second later because of Hugo.

"Shh, it will be okay. You're the strongest woman I know. And Zeke knows that. He'll come around," Nora says.

I am strong.

But Zeke won't come around. That hurt doesn't go away.

The good news is I've finally got the missing piece back

from Hugo. Any love I once felt for him is now gone. The bad news is all of my heart belongs to Zeke Kane—a man who vowed to stop protecting it. A man who gave me one moment of vulnerability, only to take away any thought of love a second later.

I was hurt by Hugo. I paid for seven years for the pain Hugo caused me. But Zeke has the power to hurt me for forever. The love I have for Zeke is different than the love I had for Hugo. The love I had for Hugo only went surface deep, but the love I have for Zeke is down to the depths of my soul.

Hugo was a slimy man looking for his next lay. Zeke, whether he admits it or not, is the most loyal man and can only do forever relationships. He's too loyal not to be with a woman who will one day become his wife.

And Zeke thinks I'm too disloyal to ever earn that title.

27

ZEKE

THE PLANE RIDE BACK TAKES a thousand hours. At least that's how the nine-hour plane ride feels.

The distance between where Siren sat on the plane and I sat was less than ten feet. But it might as well have been an ocean between us. Neither of us looked at each other. Or acknowledged each other. We acted like strangers.

A complete one-eighty from how we behaved on the first flight.

But if I thought the plane ride was long, it was the easy part. Once we said goodbye to Nora, the truck ride back to my house was ten times longer.

Again we didn't speak. Or look at each other. We sat in silence. But that didn't mean we both weren't thinking about the other.

I'm missing something. I know I am. But what?

In the bathroom in Paris, Siren would have told me anything. She would have told me the entire truth. She would have vowed to be on my side—declared her love forever.

When we were making love, it felt like that's what we were doing.

But the second we stepped out into the bedroom, everything changed. I no longer felt like Siren and I were on the same team. We were all on different teams. All fighting for ourselves.

Then Siren chose to save Hugo.

Is that her thing? She just likes saving people? Even scum like Hugo?

Or does she still love him? She said she didn't, not anymore, but I can't figure out why she won't let me kill him, especially after what he did to her that night.

A part of me says I should have done it. I don't take orders from Siren. And Hugo deserved to die more than most men I've killed.

But I looked in her damn eyes, the same soft, warm eyes that fell apart at the pain he did to her. The same eyes that held my entire world when I made love to her. And I couldn't betray those eyes.

So Hugo lives, for now.

I need to know why she saved him, for my own sanity. But I have to protect myself. She can't keep hurting me. And whether for self-preservation or because she's devious, she keeps lying to me by hiding the truth. She may not lie with her words, but she lies by hiding the truth, which is just as vile.

I sling my bag over my shoulder when we get to my house. Siren waits for me to unlock the front door before entering, which is unlike her. But she doesn't wait for me to invite her in once I open the door.

I head to the fridge and pull out stuff to make a sandwich. I'm starving. Before I realize what I'm doing, I make one for Siren.

She sits down at my dining room table with her laptop and two coffees. *When did she make those?*

I put one of the sandwiches in front of her. Then I sit down kitty-corner to her with my own sandwich and drink the coffee she placed in front of me.

Neither of us thanks the other for getting the food and coffee. Our eyes both betray us, saying our thanks anyway.

I pull out Mr. Martinez's stolen phone.

We stare at our electronic devices for a second as we drink some of the coffee and eat part of the sandwiches. Then we get to work, still in silence. Siren on her laptop. Me on the phone. Both of us doing business without words.

I pull up Mr. Martinez's bank account on the phone. It has over a billion dollars in it. She picked our target well.

She looks at it and types some more into the computer, probably pulling up Julian's bank information so we can make the transfer.

Her job is easy since Julian gave her the information needed to make a transfer.

Suddenly her mouth drops open.

"I, um…" she speaks for the first time.

"What?" I ask, my first word to her since leaving Hugo in the Parisian hotel room.

"Julian gave me an empty bank account to make the transfer into. But I was nosy and had some time on the plane, so I've been working on hacking into his main bank accounts and…"

She turns the computer screen so I can see what she's looking at.

"Holy shit," I say, my jaw dropping to the floor and my tired eyes widening at the sight of the number on the screen.

It's a huge number. Like Bill Gates big. No, bigger. Like Jeff Bezos big—no, double that.

What is Julian Reed up to? Or better yet, who is Julian Reed? He's not the small-time drug dealer turned human trafficker I thought he was. This man is loaded. He has more money than my old boss Enzo Black ever dreamed of having.

Julian is more dangerous than I realized. *Has he been playing me all along?* He sure as hell doesn't need the billion dollars we are transferring to him.

I look at Siren, studying her reaction. She's a good actress, but the shock on her face looks real enough. And she's doing more than just staring; she's running her hand through her hair, she's grabbing at her chest like she's having a panic attack. I don't know how you fake that.

"Siren? Are you okay?" I ask, standing as she does, prepared for her to faint or be sick.

She nods. "Um...can you finish the transfer?"

"Yes, but—"

"Good. Make the transfer, and then tell Julian we finished the task." She starts walking toward the door.

"Where are you going?"

"I'm sorry. I have to go," she grabs the door with sorrow and fear in her eyes. She's gone, without a word or explanation. I'm left to deal with finishing the job, the shock of this new information about Julian, and the unanswered questions that always arise with Siren. For every answer I get, I end up with more questions.

I stare back at the computer. I need to finish. Transfer the money into the empty account and act like I don't know Julian has money. I need to make sure Lucy is safe ASAP.

Then I need to do more digging into Julian Reed. Because if he's after Enzo Black and our family, I'm not sure we are going to be able to stop him.

28

SIREN

EVERYTHING I THOUGHT I knew was a lie.

Everything.

EVERYTHING.

I thought Julian Reed was an evil man.

I thought he was a drug dealer.

Sometimes a human trafficker.

I thought he made above-average money, more than any normal person needed to survive.

I thought he had power, but that it was limited.

All of those facts are wrong. None of them are the whole truth.

Julian Reed is worse than evil. I always thought of him as the devil, but now I know he's the richest devil in all of history.

He may be a drug dealer, but you don't make that kind of money selling drugs from a tiny island.

He may sell people, but not billions of dollars worth of people.

And Julian's power isn't limited; it's far-reaching. He may

be the most powerful man on the planet. If another person has more money than him, I've never heard of it.

How?

Why?

How did I not know Julian Reed has this much money and power? Because he doesn't act like it. He acts like he's just growing his business. Like he isn't the most powerful man in the world.

Maybe it's because he isn't? Maybe he's just holding onto the money for his boss?

But Julian Reed doesn't act like he has a boss. I don't think he could handle having a boss. But I also didn't think the man was capable of having this much money.

It doesn't matter what I assumed. It doesn't matter that Julian manipulated me as much as I manipulate other men.

I need to put all of that aside. I have more important things to do now that I know this information.

I need to find out everything I can before Julian realizes I know about his wealth, which could only mean a few hours with the resources he probably has.

Most importantly, I need to find a way to protect as many people as I can. And I know exactly who I'm starting with.

29

ZEKE

"The billion dollars is in your account," I say to Julian. We are standing on his back deck while Julian smokes a cigar and looks out at the view of the ocean. This isn't his usual spot, but it is a particularly nice day. I guess I understand why we are outside enjoying the sun.

But I can't enjoy anything. Not until I protect the people I love.

"Excellent work. You did that quickly. Three days? Impressive."

"You aren't even going to check your account balance?"

"Aria sent me the bank report earlier today. I already checked."

Siren.

I haven't seen her in twenty-four hours. *Has she been here this whole time? Or did Julian send her on a mission?*

"What did you do to Lucy? Where is she?" I ask, trying to keep the anger out of my voice. I need answers, not revenge.

After I transferred the money, I immediately got in contact with my guys closest to Seattle. They went in search of Lucy. But she was already gone—someone got there first.

I should have moved her sooner; the second Siren gave me her address. I didn't want to disrupt her life unless I had to, but it was the wrong decision.

Julian puffs on his damn cigar. I want to shove it down his throat and suffocate him with it.

"Seattle, as far as I know. I brought my team back when Aria agreed to the date. I kept my word and haven't gone after Lucy. Once I make a promise, I always keep it." He exhales a perfect circle of smoke.

I pull my gun out and aim it at him. I'm done being nice. I need answers.

"Where is Lucy?" I ask again.

He shakes his head. "Shoot me, and you'll never find out. If you want me to find Lucy for you, we can make a deal of our own."

Julian doesn't seem the least bit scared at the sight of my gun. I've threatened him too many times without actually killing him.

Dammit.

I lower my gun. "I'm done making deals with you. I've made my last deal. Two down. Three to go."

"Ready for the next round?" Julian asks with a grin. He knows I'm not ready until I figure out where Lucy is.

I ignore him and walk out. I'll get every contact I can find that has nothing to do with Enzo Black looking for Lucy. But I suspect they won't find her. Whoever took her hid her well.

I walk out of the house toward my truck when I spot Siren heading toward Julian's house.

It all clicks.

"Did you move Lucy? Did you take her?" I ask, my voice threatening. No one touches Lucy without paying the consequences. Not even Siren.

"Yes," she answers without hesitation.

I grab Siren's arms and push her against the side of my truck.

"What the hell? Why?"

She winces but doesn't immediately answer.

"Where is she?" I ask, almost losing it.

"I can't tell you the—"

But I don't let her finish. The second she says she can't tell me, Siren becomes dead to me.

Siren told me her truth; now it's my turn.

"I'll kill you if you hurt her. I'll kill you if she gets hurt because of you."

I release her.

"The only reason you aren't dead right now is so I can torture you to find out where she is."

The words are my truth. I promised Lucy a long time ago I'd kill for her. I never thought that I'd have to kill someone I care about, though.

As I speak the words, as I hear them, as I see the defiance in Siren's eyes, I know my words aren't true. I can't kill Siren. But I can't break my vow to Lucy either.

I don't have a choice. Someday soon, I won't be able to protect them both. I'm going to have to choose. And for a split second, I'm not sure which woman will survive.

30

SIREN

I moved Lucy. Not for whatever devious reasons Zeke is accusing me of.

I moved Lucy to keep her safe. I didn't have a choice. I don't trust Julian, not anymore, not with anything. Not even with his promises.

Lucy needed to be moved. She needed to be moved securely and quickly and with as few people as possible. She needed to be moved to the furthest corner of the earth. She needed to be moved by the best people.

Zeke could have moved her. But he didn't. I know he was preparing to. To avoid contacting his old world and Enzo Black, he was going to have her moved by people that have no connection to his family. I'm sure they are good men, but not the best.

This job required the best, and even that might not be enough to hide her from Julian forever.

I can't tell Zeke where she is. Not here. Not when Julian is listening to our conversations. Not even in his house where I'm sure there are more security systems monitoring us than either one of us wants to admit. Sure, we both found some bugs, but there's more we haven't found.

Zeke said he would kill me. If it came down to Lucy or me, he would kill me. I understand. That's what love does. It makes you crazy.

If it comes down to Lucy or me, I hope he does choose Lucy. That's what love has done to me. I want Zeke to get his happily ever after with the love of his life, even if that isn't with me.

And I'd rather be dead than live in a world without Zeke.

I can't keep living in a world where three men try to control me—Julian, Hugo, and Zeke.

I may not be able to do anything about Julian right now.

And I don't want to do anything about Zeke right now.

But I can do something about Hugo.

Maybe doing something big out in the open, letting Zeke in on one part of the truth so he understands the sacrifice I'm making for him, will be enough to get him to trust me with Lucy, at least for a moment.

"Lucy's safe. You don't have to believe me. Go search for her if you must, but she's safe. You're not the only person willing to protect people we love," I say, coming the closest yet to telling Zeke that I love him.

Zeke shakes his head. "I'm tired of the lies, Siren."

"It's not a lie."

"I can't trust you. You know the stupid game we play—truth or sin? There is no truth in that game. It's always sin, even when you choose truth. You've never told me the truth. You're never going to tell me the truth. And at this point, even if you tell me the truth, I won't believe you."

I start walking, hoping Zeke will follow me. He does. He's not finished with this conversation.

We walk half a mile into the jungle on the edge of Julian's property. It's not remote enough to tell Zeke the truth about Lucy. Julian could still hear. And as Zeke said, I could tell him the truth, and he wouldn't believe me anyway.

But we're far enough away for me to do this.

I pull out my knife.

Zeke laughs. "What? You brought me to the jungle so you can kill me?"

I turn the knife around, holding onto the blade, while holding the handle out to Zeke. He takes it.

Then I turn my back to him and lift my hair up so he can see the three names on my neck.

The first name is Hugo's. The first name was written with love. I wanted a tattoo of Hugo's name; I was so in love with him. The last two—Julian's and Zeke's—were written out of loyalty and pain. Someday all the names will be gone. But today, I get to remove one with Zeke's help.

Zeke reaches out and touches the names slowly with his fingers, unable to resist.

Shivers course through me, but I remain still. I will not let him know how his touch affects me.

"Cross out Hugo's name with the knife," I command.

Zeke doesn't move.

"Zeke, cross out Hugo's name."

He pauses for a second, and then he carefully thumbs the names on the back of my neck before pressing the cold of the metal against my base.

I suck in a breath at the same time he slices through the name. I've never wanted to feel pain as much as I do right now. I needed to feel his name ripped from my body.

I feel strong.

Powerful.

I know exactly what I'm doing—taking my life back, one man at a time. I will own my own life, my own name, and my own heart again. Zeke's name will be the hardest to cross out, but someday, I'll cross it out. When I deliver Zeke safely to Lucy, back to his own world.

Zeke blows on the wound gently, and then he ties my hair up with a scrunchie from his arm, keeping my hair from getting into the fresh wound.

I bite my lip to keep from smiling. *How can he be so kind to me? So protective? So caring?*

My heart is doing flips at the small gesture.

I turn and face him.

"Why did I just scar your neck? Why did I cross through Hugo's name?"

"Because I'm finally ready to divorce him."

He gasps.

"Once I file, once the agreement of the prenup is complete, then you can at least know one truth."

31

ZEKE

SIREN STARTS to walk away but stops. She looks at me, and I don't see fear like I expect. *I see hope.*

"You're my anchor, Zeke. Don't forget that."

I blink rapidly, not understanding.

"What does that mean?"

She smiles softly, as if the secret her words are hiding is precious and nice instead of what they really are—just one more lie.

"It means you're my strong, unmoving force. You keep me grounded. You ensure I live, even when I should die. You are the one stable thing in my life. You can make sure that I come back—not by saving me, but by never letting me truly go in the first place. You anchor me here."

Her words tell me everything and nothing.

But they keep her here for a second longer—another second for me to come to my senses and realize what she's doing.

At first, I thought she stayed married because she loved him. Maybe she did once, but that love has been lost. I don't know what the prenup she signed says, but it must be bad if it keeps her married to Hugo. Whatever she must do in order to get the divorce they both want will hurt her. And hurting her will hurt me.

"Don't..." I reach out, as if my hand will stop her. It won't. Nothing will now that's she made up her mind.

I'm torn. I want her to divorce him. I want her to be rid of him. I want to have a sliver of hope that we could have a future if we ever forgave each other for all the lying.

But I don't want her to leave. I don't want her to get hurt.

"What does the prenup say?" I ask, scared of what she's going to say.

She sighs. "It says that soon I'm going to be stronger than I've ever been. It says that soon I'll feel a little freer than I felt before."

And then she's gone. Running away from me.

I could chase her.

I could demand she tell me.

I could keep her here until she tells me the truth.

But I won't. If you love someone, you set them free. *Do I love her?*

Maybe.

Definitely.

Is it healthy?

Hell no.

Will our love last?

Doubtful. I doubt both of us will still be breathing a year from now.

Does it stop me from chasing after her?

Absolutely not.

I run once I realize what I want. Her unhurt. Her alive. I don't want her in pain. I don't want her dead. I need to find her. I can't let her go.

But Siren knows the jungle better than I do. By the time I make it back to my truck, she's already gone.

It won't stop me from chasing after her. It won't stop me from saving her if I have to.

I vowed I would stop saving her, but I can't.

If there is a chance I was wrong about her this whole time, if there's a chance we can heal the wounds we've caused in each other's hearts, then I'll never forgive myself for not saving her.

32

SIREN

I MEET Hugo at the house we technically own together, but I've never spent more than a night in it since we got married. The house is small, modest. He doesn't stay on this island often. Just when he wants something from me.

Like now.

The anger flares in his eyes as he stands in front of the front door.

"You have some balls showing up here," he says.

I raise an eyebrow. "This is my house."

"You stole from my parents," Hugo growls. It's not as deep or sexy as when Zeke growls. Hugo bares his teeth during his growl, making it frightening.

"Yea, what are you going to do about it?" He can't do anything to me.

"I was going to add it to your debt and make you pay every penny back with interest," he yells.

"You can't prove I stole the money. Even Julian will back me up. I don't owe you anything."

He huffs. "Then I'll kill that boyfriend of yours."

I laugh. "Not if he kills you first."

Fear—I see the fear in his eyes. It gives me satisfaction, and I smirk a little, trying to be brave for the next step. In a few seconds, Hugo's going to be the one with the smirk, not me.

"What are you doing here, Aria?"

"I'm giving you what you want."

"Which is what?"

"A divorce."

The words alone scare the crap out of me. I'm giving up so much. Possibly everything. I'm chancing everything by divorcing Hugo. It's necessary.

It's the only way to gain everything.

"I don't believe you," Hugo says.

"Let me inside."

Hugo stares at me, trying to understand why I'm doing this. The reason he wrote this in the prenup was because, at the time, he wanted me to stay married to him forever. He thought with this prenup, I'd never divorce him. I'd be his forever. Trapped in a binding contract. He could flaunt it over me for the rest of my life.

Hugo doesn't really want a divorce. He wants control over me. It's all he's wanted since I was eighteen.

He's about to get one last drop of power over me, then nothing, forever.

He marches inside, and I follow him through the house he clearly hasn't kept up. The house is dingy. Clothes and trash clutter most of the rooms. Hugo is headed for one room, in particular, a room he made into an office.

He heads to a filing cabinet and unlocks it, pulling open the top drawer roughly, almost pulling the entire cabinet down. His eyes lock with mine, glaring over the cabinet. Then he's searching through the papers until he finds what he's looking for.

He flings the papers on the desk.

"Read it again. And then tell me you still want a divorce," he says.

I feel my hands tremble. But I fist them and then open them, forcing my body to settle. I'm making the right decision—the only decision. I'm stronger than what Hugo has planned.

I can do this. I can win.

But what if I don't?

I told Zeke not to save me.

Julian might, just to keep his best asset close.

But what if neither of them comes? What if I can't save myself?

Then I'll die happy, no longer married to this asshole.

I flip through the papers quickly, reading the crucial part again, trying to decipher any hidden meaning of the words I haven't realized before. But I find no hidden meaning.

The prenup is on top, along with divorce papers Hugo had drawn up in case I ever wanted a divorce.

"Got a pen?" I ask.

Hugo laughs, likes he thinks I'm bluffing. He thinks I won't really sign the papers.

He continues to chuckle as he opens the desk drawer, facing me head-on. He pulls out a pen and holds it out to me.

He's not going to make any of this easy—not one second.

My heart thumps wildly. My hands clam up. Goosebumps form on my arms. There is no hiding my fear from Hugo. Not this time.

Slowly, I take the pen from him. It doesn't matter that he knows I'm scared. What matters is that I sign the papers. That is my moment of strength.

I flip to the last page, and I sign my name.

Hugo's jaw hits the floor as I toss the papers in his face. "Do your worst," I say.

33

ZEKE

It's been one week since Siren left.

Vanished, more like it. I can't find her anywhere. Not a Julian's. Nowhere near the compound. Nowhere on the island. I've even called my contacts to start looking for her, but they can't find her either.

Siren isn't the only person who vanished. Lucy is still missing.

I've done everything short of contacting Enzo Black to find her.

My only comfort is that I don't think Julian knows where they are either.

At least, I don't think so. But I'm out of options. Julian may not care where Lucy is, but he cares about Siren.

I march into his office as his butler tries to stop me.

"Julian," I say as I kick open his door.

"I'm so sorry, sir. He just stormed in," the butler says.

"It's okay, Hanson. Zeke is always welcome here."

The butler leaves in a scurry.

"What do you want?" Julian asks, reading his newspaper.

"Tell me what the prenup said," I say.

His eyes draw up over the newspaper. And he grins. "I told you to ask Aria. It's not my truth to tell."

"I would, except she's disappeared. Know anything about that?"

He scoffs. "She'll turn up again. She made a vow to me. Trust me, she'll never break it."

I glare at him, ripping the newspaper from his hands. "You really think Siren cares about a vow she made to you to save a man she hates?"

"Yes, because you don't understand who Aria is. You don't understand what she's done."

He doesn't realize what's happened. He doesn't realize what Siren's done.

"What did the prenup say?" I ask, my voice gravely and full of anger.

"Why?"

"Because she signed the divorce papers."

"Shit," Julian jumps up faster than I've ever seen him. He's on his phone in a second, barking orders to his men to go search for Siren.

For the first time, Julian and I just got on the same side, if only for a brief second.

34

SIREN

"He's here," Hugo says, glancing out our hotel window. After I signed the divorce papers, we went to Portugal. Apparently, Hugo wasn't too surprised I signed the papers because he had a whole plan already in place. He put everything in motion with one phone call.

I sit on the edge of the hotel bed. It's a cheap room, and the bed dips wherever I sit on it.

"It's time to go," Hugo says.

"Why?" I ask, hoping for one last chance to convince Hugo not to do this.

He stares at me—really stares—like he's taking a mental picture to remember this moment forever. And that terrifies me. If he's taking a picture, then this is goodbye for real. He doesn't think I'm going to survive this. He doesn't think I'll be coming back next week to chew him out.

"You shouldn't have stolen the money from my parents," he says.

"Maybe not. They aren't bad people per se, they just raised a horrible son."

Hugo frowns.

"But that's not why you are doing this, Hugo. That's not why you added the provision to the prenup that allowed you to do this. Why did you?"

There is a knock at our hotel room door. My time is up.

"Because you were mine. Mine to love. Mine to keep. Mine to hold. And I knew if I had to ever let you go, this was the only way I could bear it."

Those were not the words I was expecting to hear. I wasn't expecting Hugo to admit that he loved me. I assumed he would be doing this for revenge and for his sick twisted pleasure.

"You don't get to claim you are selling me for love," I say.

"No, but love is the reason all the same."

Hugo opens the door, and a man walks in. This isn't the man I'm being sold to. This is his henchman.

"This the girl?" The man asks.

Hugo nods.

"Wow, an obedient one. You don't even need ropes or handcuffs."

Hugo shakes his head sadly. "She's the least obedient person I know. She will fight harder than any woman your master has ever bought. And she will burn the castle down with her. She's not going to submit. She's going to destroy you. Only if your master is smart about controlling her will you have a chance against her. But even then, she will eventually win. She always wins."

Our eyes lock as he speaks so highly of me.

"Then why is she submitting now?" the man asks.

"Because this is the only way to get what she wants. And she doesn't fear being sold. She doesn't fear you. She fears nothing, because she is stronger than you could ever imagine," Hugo says.

"Her name?" the man asks, continuing to talk about me like I'm not here.

I wait for Hugo to say Aria, or maybe bitch, or cunt, if he's in a particularly foul mood. Instead, he says, "Siren."

It feels like a truce. He's admitting who I really am and who I deserve to be with. That I need to be free of him. That I belong with Zeke.

"Is she ready?" the man asks.

"Almost," Hugo walks over to me and holds out his hand, demanding me to turn over my gun.

I do. Then Hugo gives me a quick pat-down. He knows I always carry more than one weapon, but when he finds the knife buried in my boot, Hugo just winks at me and lets me keep it.

I have a weapon, for now at least.

Why is Hugo being nice to me?

Surprising my further, Hugo wraps his arms around me, hugging me. "I could have loved you forever, but that wouldn't have been fair to you. You deserve someone worthy of you."

I blink, rapidly as he pulls away and walks over to the divorce papers. He signs them, knowing I'll keep my word and willingly go with the man. At least until I get to his car, then all bets are off.

"Why?" I ask one last time.

Hugo smiles at me.

"He will only come if you are in danger. You two need all the help you can get in the love department," Hugo says. Then he slings his bag over his shoulder, and walks out the door.

I'm left stunned by Hugo's admission. Maybe the prenup was originally to ensure I never divorced him, but now he's keeping to the contract to push Zeke and me together.

Unbelievable.

It's not true. Hugo is an evil, manipulative asshole.

An asshole I once loved.

But an asshole all the same. A man I won't think of again after today.

Hugo is wrong about Zeke coming for me. I told him not to, and he'll listen. This won't bring Zeke and me closer together. Even if it did, this isn't how I want us to end up together. I want us to choose each other, not be scared of losing each other.

After Hugo leaves, my purchaser's henchman opens the door, and three other men run inside with guns.

Apparently, Hugo had already warned them I wasn't going to go with them easy. I'm a fighter.

They give me no choice but to surrender, binding my hands and ankles. Then I'm dragged to the back of a truck where the three men surround me.

Now doesn't seem like the best time to escape. But I will escape. And I will kill every one of these men.

A truck ride, a plane ride, and another car ride later, I'm dragged into a house and thrown in the basement.

I can save myself. I can escape.

But when I see a dozen eyes staring back at me, I realize it's not just myself that needs saving. I wasn't counting on having to save someone else too.

35

HUGO

SELLING Aria hurt more than I thought it would. I knew I would have to do it someday, even when I added that provision to the prenup. Aria was never really mine. I thought being able to control her would feel like she was mine, even when she stopped loving me.

But it doesn't.

I have no control.

I knew when we said our wedding vows that Aria was too good for me. I knew this is how our marriage would end. But I wasn't prepared for what signing the divorce papers would feel like.

It destroyed me singing my name next to Aria's, telling the world that I no longer care about this woman, and admitting Aria is no longer mine.

In reality, she hasn't been mine for years.

Aria will escape. I won't be here when she does. Being sold is temporary. Aria can never be contained by a man. Never be owned.

Zeke Kane might be the only man who can tame her.

And even he will have to fight constantly to keep her his. Eventually, she will get free of even him.

Aria Torres is invincible. She's independent and kind and selfless. And she deserved better.

But so did I.

Aria was the only woman who could give me what I needed. But what I asked for was too great. I needed forgiveness, in spite of who I was. I needed to be forgiven again and again.

Yes, I fucked up. I cheated on her. I broke Aria's heart.

But Aria is forgiveness. She is kindness. So I thought she would forgive me.

We were kids when we got married. I didn't understand what marriage was. I was a drug addict. I was constantly fucked up and made a lot of bad decisions.

The only good decision I made was marrying Aria.

I loved her desperately, but I cost her everything. Ten years of her life she gave to save me. And I paid her back by cheating on her. That isn't something even the highest angel can forgive.

I don't regret falling in love with Aria, because she saved my life more than she knows...

My heart is racing, jonesing for another hit. I need it. I'm desperate. I need a hit right now. My legs are shaking, I'm sweaty, and I can't get enough oxygen in my lungs.

I need the drugs. It's been too long since my last hit.

I bought drugs meant to be sold, but instead, me and my friends used them. Not this time. This time, I'm selling them and only using a little bit. I just need one hit, then I'll be able to function again.

I'm supposed to meet the buyer here, on the edge of this

sea town. I'm so damn tired of the sea salt smell and the humid, sticky air. Beach towns are overrated.

I turn down a road and into the alleyway where I met him last time, but I don't see him.

Am I early?

Late?

I don't know. I don't have a watch. Or a phone.

I have no way to figure out if he's coming or already left.

But I'm not going anywhere. For one thing, the alleyway is spinning.

I need to sit down.

So I do.

"Ow," a high pitched voice says.

I stumble over and look down at what I stepped on—an angel.

Did I die?

I must have.

The girl smiles up at me when she sees my reaction. *Yep, I'm definitely dead. No girl looks as sweet as her.*

She's leaning against the wall, playing with something in her hand. Even though she's sitting on the dirty ground in the alleyway next to a trash can, she looks clean and smells like flowers.

"You should sit down; you don't look so well," she says.

I slump to the floor next to her.

"Are you sick?" she asks with big eyes.

I nod. I'm always sick. Except when I'm high, which seems to be less and less these days.

"Here," she says, removing her denim jacket and draping it over my shoulders.

I stare at her with bug eyes.

"You are shaking. You must be cold. The jacket will help."

I nod. It does help. Although not as much as a hit of heroin would.

"What are you doing here?" I ask her, still assuming I'm dead.

Her beautiful bright smile drops. "Hiding."

"From what?"

"Not what, who," she answers. Her eyes drift down the alleyway, looking lost in a cloud of gloom.

Okay, so she's a dark angel. She hides behind her pretty eyelashes and big smile, but I can see the darkness now. She's had a rough past, same as me.

I study her closer and realize she's young. Seventeen, maybe eighteen.

She's either running from her parents or a boyfriend.

"Have a boyfriend?" I ask.

She shakes her head, and I have my answer—she's running from her parents.

"What's your name?"

"Aria Torres."

"I'm Hugo Martinez."

She nods, giving me a polite smile. She tucks her hair behind her ear, and that's when I see it, the blueness around her eye.

If I was in a better place, I'd get up and run after her dad. I'd kill him for touching such a sweet angel. But since I can barely keep myself sitting upright, I don't think I can manage chasing down a grown man.

Aria reaches over and grabs a bottle I didn't notice before. She takes a sip of the beer and then hands it to me. "Want some?"

I take the bottle, the alcohol barely addressing my jitters, but I appreciate the taste and gesture.

"What are you doing in an alleyway like this, Aria? You could be enjoying the beach."

"The same reason you are."

I frown. This girl should be doing nothing I'm doing. I lean my head back against the brick wall behind us.

"So, what do you like doing for fun, Aria?"

Please don't say drink or drugs. You're better than that. Give me hope.

She frowns. "I don't know. I don't do anything for fun."

"Well, if you could, what would you do?"

She thinks for a moment, scrunching her nose. "Sing."

It seems like an admission she's never made to anyone else before. But she made it to me. I feel my jittery heart do strange things—like flip for this girl.

"What do you like to sing?"

"I don't know. I've never tried singing before."

"You want to sing, but you've never tried it before? How do you know you are any good?"

She smiles. "I don't. Don't you have dreams you've never tried before? Skiing, surfing, painting?"

I don't tell her that I've done all of those things. I grew up privileged. That doesn't mean that the darkness didn't find me, too, just like this girl who has nothing. This girl, who has been beaten, abused, and yet she still smiles. She still has hope.

"Well, I think it's about time."

"Time for what?"

"Time that you sing."

She frowns. "But I don't know how."

I laugh. "Yes, you do. Singing isn't something that has to be taught. At least not at first. Sure, to get good at singing on key and harmonizing and stuff, you might need lessons, but you don't have to be good to start singing. You just sing."

"Okay, if you don't need lessons, then you sing," she says with a raised eyebrow.

I walked right into that one.

I think for a moment, trying to come up with something to sing. Then I open my mouth and sing 'Moves Like Jagger.'

Siren smiles. "Did you write that?"

I frown. "No, it's Maroon 5. Haven't you heard it on the radio?"

She blushes. "My parents don't have a radio."

Oh.

Shit.

"I'm sorry, I shouldn't have pushed you."

But then she opens her mouth and starts singing. A song I've never heard before. One I'm sure she's written herself.

You hurt me.
Destroyed me.
Made me turn to darkness to survive you.
The pull is too great.
I can't resist your temptation.
It's the only way to survive you.
Even though it destroys me.
And yet, I still love you.

My mouth falls open as she sings. I was wrong about everything. This girl can sing. She doesn't need lessons or practice. This girl could be on the radio right now if she wanted to be. If the right person listened to her, the pain in her life would vanish.

But that's what makes her voice so special—the pain behind it. The life experience.

"It was horrible, wasn't it?" she asks, her voice timid.

I shake my head. "That was the most hauntingly beautiful thing I've ever heard."

She swallows hard, and her mouth goes dry as she stares at me like I'm someone to awe.

Then—an electricity I've never felt with a woman before. I need to touch her. She seems to need it too.

We've found something here, connected in a way neither of us was expecting. We are two lost souls in need of saving. Maybe we can save each other.

I touch her cheek.

She touches my chest.

And then we kiss.

Our lips brush. Our tongues tease. And the beautiful thing that is Aria encompasses me. *I'm hers—forever.*

I don't know how I'm going to hold onto something so beautiful. So precious. So forgiving. But I'm going to try.

Finally, I see it—the needle next to her leg. And I see the darkness in her eyes as I kiss her. She's facing the same monster as I am.

The pull of drugs.

She's not shaking like I am, and she doesn't have needle marks all up and down her arms like I do. She can still be saved from the deepest layer of darkness.

I can save her. I can protect her. And maybe her goodness, her kindness, her ability to forgive will be enough... because I already know I'm going to have to ask for her forgiveness.

My love wasn't enough to protect her.

Her forgiveness wasn't enough to save our marriage.

Love isn't enough to protect against darkness.

What I did was unforgivable.

When I was planning our life together, I forgot one thing —Aria fell in love with me too. And love makes people do unpredictable things. Aria is the strongest person I know, but I broke her heart. I didn't realize how fragile it was since everything else about her is strong.

I know what's coming, and I deserve it. I need it to happen. Despite everything, I still love Aria. But she's no longer Aria. Aria is gone. She left the second I shattered her heart.

She's Siren now. She finally found a man worthy of her. I just hope my plan works. I hope the pain brings them together, like it did us. And I hope, unlike us, they cherish their love instead of letting it destroy them.

But I better not be here to watch it happen, because Aria isn't the only one with a fragile heart. I can't watch her get her happily ever after, while I'm the reason ours ended.

36

ZEKE

JULIAN DRIVES me to Hugo's house. I must be crazy to trust Julian, even for a second, to get her back. I don't have a choice—Julian knows Hugo and Siren's history better than I do.

"There," Julian says when we pull up in front of a small beach house on the far end of the island.

I pull my gun out. *Hugo's a dead man if he sold Siren. A dead man.*

Julian pulls a gun out as well. I've never seen him get his hands dirty, never seen him wield a gun, but for Siren, he will. He loves her, which is the only reason I brought him along. He'd die, before he'd let her die.

He may have been a good actor. He may have acted like he would kill her if I didn't behave, but no way can Julian kill Siren. Just like there is no way I can kill her. There is just something about her that lures men in. Only she can decide if we get to live or die.

We march up to Hugo's front door. I pound loudly on the door, my gun in hand, and Julian standing on my right.

Slowly, Hugo opens the door. We don't give him time to

talk. We both ambush him back into his house until he's sitting in a chair in the center of his living room with both our guns aimed at his forehead.

The house is a mess. There's trash and empty alcohol bottles everywhere. That isn't what has me worried, though. The track marks on his arms worry me. The redness in his eyes. The brokenness. The needles on the coffee table.

Hugo is high. Who knows if we will be able to get answers from him.

"Where is Siren?" I ask.

"Who?" Hugo asks.

"Aria, your wife. Where is she?" Julian asks.

"Oh, her," Hugo's head drops, and I swear he's seconds away from passing out, puking, or keeling over dead. I'm just not sure which.

He's no longer the man I knew before. He's not the man who would fight for Siren, the man who would make threats. This man is empty, broken.

Julian kicks him in the leg. "Wake up! Where is Aria?"

Hugo's head drops again, and he shakes his head.

I study him, trying to figure out how to play this. How to get the information we need? We need to know where Siren is. If he doesn't tell us, it could take us days to find her instead of hours. I don't want her with another man for any longer than she has to be.

"Where is she?" I ask, calmer.

Hugo looks at me in the eyes, and for a second, I see clarity. He looks over at Julian, and his eyes get cloudy again.

"Julian, make him some coffee or something. He's so high he won't be able to think straight."

Julian doesn't like taking orders, but he wants Siren back just like I do. He reluctantly marches into the kitchen to make coffee.

I squat down in front of Hugo. "Who did you sell her to?"

"Northern Spain. The number is in my pocket," Hugo answers me.

I exhale a deep breath as I reach into his front pocket and find a note. I have her location and a phone number. *I can find her. I can save her.*

Hugo grabs my shirt, holding me close. "Don't break her heart. It's fragile. Protect it at all costs."

I frown, not understanding.

"Promise me!" His voice gets louder.

I don't know why I'm making promises to Hugo, but I am. "I promise."

Hugo grabs my gun and aims it at his heart.

I realize what's happened—Hugo's hurting. His heart is broken. *He really did love her.*

Three men.

Hugo.

Julian.

And me.

We've all fallen for her. Siren's love is the kind that consumes you. It's all any of us can think about—loving her. She's strong, independent, and secretive—a true siren with the power to kill us all. She just has to decide if she wants any of us alive.

Divorcing Hugo was the final straw. He lost. And now he can't survive without her. It hurts too much. She destroyed him.

I don't understand their love story, but I don't doubt now that they loved each other. I don't doubt that he loved her more than she loved him. Even though she traded ten years of her life to save him, he still loved her more. And in the end, it was his demise.

"Do it," Hugo says.

I look at him closer. He's already dying. He's gaunt, just bones. If I don't kill him, the drugs will. For a moment, I feel sorry for him. Ultimately, he simply wasn't strong enough to keep her love.

Am I?

No. I'm not sure any man is.

But that's a discussion for later. For now, I get to kill a man who hurt Siren. I get to get her vengeance. Hugo may love her, but he still sold her. He cheated on her. He nearly raped her. He locked her into a marriage when she was never his to begin with.

The only way to keep Siren's love is to let her be herself, let her be free. Let her be Siren and hope your love is enough. You can't cage her in like Hugo did.

You can't trap her into vows like Julian does.

You can't force her to tell you the truth when she's not ready like I do.

I don't know how Siren needs to be loved, but all three of us are doing a horrible job. All three of us are going to end up dying with a broken heart, just like Hugo.

I consider letting him die slowly and painfully, but it's not my style. And I don't think it's what Siren would want. She loved him once. She wants him to die honorably, before he loses himself completely.

He closes his eyes, welcoming death. I let him die with a bullet in his heart, putting him out of his misery.

Julian enters when he hears the gunshot.

"What the hell? You killed him before you found out where Aria is?"

"No, I found out where she is."

"Where?"

"This is where our partnership ends." I shoot him in the

shoulder, not enough to kill him, although I want to desperately. I'm afraid he's working for a more powerful man—the one whose money that really is. I don't want to piss that man off by killing his number two, not at least until I know who he is.

Then I leave. I know where to find Siren. I just hope I'm not too late. And I hope I'm doing the right thing by saving her. If I know Siren, she'll most likely shoot me for saving her.

37
———

SIREN

I can do this. *I can escape. I can save all these women.*

Three men drag me in chains to a grand room, and suddenly I'm not so sure.

No, don't doubt yourself. You've been in worse situations before. You destroy men. Manipulate your new owner just like you do every other man.

"You can go," the man sitting in a large chair says to my guards.

"But, sir—"

"Unchain her, then leave," his voice is loud and booming. It's meant to scare me. It doesn't, but it drives some fear into his men.

They fumble with the chains around my wrists and ankles.

And then finally, they leave. It's just me and him—the man who bought me.

I grin. *This will be too easy.*

No, if I was just trying to free myself, it would be easy. This is harder, saving six other women.

"Who are you?" I ask, wanting to know the name of the man I plan on destroying.

"Bishop," he answers. His answer surprises me. He doesn't tell me to call him mister or master. For all I know, Bishop is his first name and not his last.

"Well, Bishop, it's nice to meet you," I say, walking over to the window to see my escape options. I'm on the third floor—jumping out the window isn't a good route.

"Is it? I would have thought it was the opposite of nice," Bishop says.

"Maybe, but I'm not like most women. I like to know who the monsters are. I don't run from them. I destroy them."

His eyes soak me in. "That you do. But I'm not like most men either."

I smirk. "All men are the same." *Except Zeke, Zeke is different. He's not a monster.*

Bishop stands and walks over to the window I've been studying. His eyes are blue, his hair blonde, and his skin fair. He doesn't look evil. The best men hide who they really are.

"You're wrong. I'm different," he says.

"How are you different?"

"I've felt pain you've never imagined. It turned me into a different man. A man who wants to see others experience similar pain."

"Don't worry about me; I have a high pain tolerance. You're not going to be able to hurt me."

He reaches out and touches my chest. "You're wrong. I know exactly how to hurt you. And I'm going to enjoy every second of it."

"And I know exactly how to hurt you."

"Oh, I hope so. I hope you are the one who can finally

hurt me because I've grown tired of the easy ones. It would be good to feel something new."

I frown. *This man is unusual.*

He snaps his fingers. A woman enters in chains being held by a man. She looks awful. She's had enough. But there's something familiar about her.

"Now, you will do exactly what I say, or Peter will torture her," Bishop says.

I close my eyes, trying to reveal nothing, but this man already has me figured out. He knows I will do anything to save someone else from being harmed.

Although, he's wrong if he thinks that will hurt me. There is only one person who could hurt me, and he's thousands of miles away.

"What do you want me to do?" I ask.

Bishop smiles. "Oh, princess. All the darkest things you can imagine."

———

There is something wrong with him—Bishop. Something fucked up in his head. Something deranged about him.

He doesn't get off raping women. He doesn't get off on control. In fact, half the time, he wants me to hurt him in the same way he's hurting me. That's what he gets off on—the pain.

Someone hurt him bad.

If I don't get out of here soon, I'm not going to be able to walk out on my own two feet.

I realize now, even I have a breaking point. Bishop has done his best in the last three days to find it. And he has.

I'm broken.

Not physically, but psychologically. I haven't slept in three days. I haven't eaten. I've barely had any water.

I'm delusional. All I see is Zeke.

Zeke...Zeke...Zeke...

He's in my head.

He's in my heart.

He's everywhere.

I can't remember if I should be running toward Zeke or away from him.

But Zeke keeps calling me. He tells me to follow him.

There is a reason I'm not supposed to go with him, but I can't remember anymore. I can't think.

I just move.

I sprint.

At least, I think I'm running.

I'm barefoot. Naked under a baggy T-shirt. My hair is a mess. My eyes are exhausted, but I keep them open. If I close them, I feel electric shocks.

Bishop enjoyed shooting electricity through my body. Seeing him do it to another woman made me beg him to give me more and her none. I can't watch others in pain.

Others! I can't run, I have to save them.

You can't save them if you are dead.

Run, get help. That's the only way to save them. You aren't strong enough on your own.

Yes, I am!

No, you're not.

The voices in my head keep fighting as I stumble through the forest. At least I think it's a forest. All I see are ghosts floating through the shadows, telling me to run.

So I run.

And run.

And run.

But I will never escape the pain. Not my own pain, that man's pain. I've never felt anything like it. I want to turn around and kill him just to end his suffering, but I can't. I have to run.

I have to escape.

I am strong enough.

I don't need a man. I don't need Zeke.

Suddenly I feel the hands grab me as I collapse. The hands aren't Zeke's hands. They are the man's—Bishop's.

"Did you enjoy your run? I enjoyed the chase." He pulls me up. "Let's get you home and fed. Then we can do that again. I quite enjoy chasing you."

I collapse in his arms. I'm not strong enough. I can't save myself. I definitely can't save the women. *I failed.*

Zeke.

Zeke isn't coming. He vowed he wouldn't, and he always keeps his word.

38

ZEKE

IT COST me everything to get Siren back.

Every penny I had.

The man Hugo sold her to is more sadistic than any man I've ever met. He would only sell her to me if I gave everything I had. He didn't care if I only had a thousand dollars in my account, he would have taken it. He just wanted me to be poor, to be worth nothing when she returned to me.

I could have fought my way in. I could have fought him, killed him. But it would have taken time, time I didn't have to get her back.

I'll kill him. Eventually, I will. But the most important thing right now is getting Siren back in my arms and away from him.

Hugo didn't tell me his name, and I still haven't learned it. Right now, his name doesn't matter. Hugo gave me the number to call. He told me she was in northern Spain.

I'm there now, waiting for Siren to be returned to me in a coffee shop.

A freaking coffee shop!

That's where he said his men would meet me.

I'm afraid he's going to double-cross me. This dark stranger hides in the shadows and enjoys playing games with me.

He won't break his word because he's watching. And he'll enjoy the show. He thinks Siren won't want me now that I'm nothing. Now that I have no money.

He's wrong.

Siren will want me. The millions in my bank account meant nothing to her. She didn't even know how much money I had. In fact, I'm pretty sure she'll love me more for giving it all away to save her.

Or she'll shoot me for not letting her save herself.

I never know which way it will go when it comes to Siren.

A car pulls up, and a woman is pushed out before it takes off.

I run to her before she collapses in the street.

"You're alive," I breathe into her hair as my tears fall.

She doesn't look too beaten up. She looks whole, but that doesn't mean I know what she's been through. It doesn't mean she didn't suffer.

I lift her up and realize how light she is. How her eyes fall closed. How her breath is weak.

"Fucker. I'm going to kill you," I vow into the darkness. *Whoever you are, you're dead for whatever you did to her.*

Siren doesn't respond to me holding her; she's too weak.

"You're safe now, I've got you," I say as I carry her to my rental truck. I will drive her to the airport where Nora is waiting for us. She hired a private jet that can make the overseas trip, as I have nothing left. No money to save Siren with. No money to bribe anyone to fly us or take care of her.

I have nothing but love to offer Siren.

I drive to the airport with Siren in my lap and my hand

on the pulse on her neck, making sure she's alive. I don't know what's wrong with her, but the waiting doctors on the plane will find out.

"Hold on, Siren. Hold on," I say.

I drive faster than I ever have before to get her to the plane. I spot Nora standing on the tarmac as I arrive. Her eyes search for Siren, still limp in my lap.

Nora grabs the door as I lift Siren out.

"Is she okay?" Nora asks.

"I don't know. She hasn't spoken. She hasn't acknowledged me at all."

Nora's eyes tell me everything. She's worried.

I carry Siren up the stairs and onto the plane where the medical team is waiting.

"How is she?" the doctor asks as I lay her on a makeshift table.

"She's unresponsive, but I felt a pulse."

"Let's get to work! Oxygen, pulse, fluids..." the doctor barks orders at his team while Nora and I stand and watch. There is nothing for us to do. We've done everything we can. Now it's up to the medical team.

"What's wrong with her?" I ask, when the flurry of excitement seems to settle down. Siren still hasn't opened her eyes.

The doctor rubs his neck. "She's definitely dehydrated, which is why she's so weak and skinny, but we couldn't find anything else physically wrong with her."

"Was she..." *Goddammit, I can't even ask.* I swallow my anger, needing to know the answer. "Was she raped?"

The doctor puts his hand on my shoulder as if to prepare me for the bad news. "I can't answer that for you. We did a rape kit, but we found no real evidence. Physically, she's fine. She could have been raped. She could have been mentally tortured. So much could have happened that I can't answer, only she can."

"How long until she wakes up?"

"Minutes, hours, days. She's exhausted and dehydrated, so her body shut down to preserve energy. I can't tell you when the body will feel rested enough to reverse course."

I nod. "Thank you, doctor."

"Sit with her. Sometimes having the person we love most close does more healing than medicine ever can."

The person we love most—I love her.

I knew it the second I realized she was sold. There was nothing I wouldn't do. *Nothing.*

I'd even hurt others I cared about or supposedly loved. Siren sucked me in and made me fall for her. I can't explain it. I'm hers. *I'm fucking hers.*

Everything else disappeared.

Lucy.

Kai.

Enzo.

My whole life—no one mattered as much as Siren. Nothing has been as complicated as loving Siren either, but I want complicated. I want messy. I want complex.

I used to think the only way to settle down was a simple life. A life where I met a simple girl who made my life easy. A woman who didn't push me to be better.

But with Siren, she makes me want to learn how to fight harder. How to be better. How to love her deeper.

I want to experience the full range of emotion. The full spectrum of life—with her. I love trying to figure her out. I love that I'm the only man capable of loving her and being loved in return without dying from heartbreak like Hugo did.

I love that this complex, strong, incredible woman chose me. Wants me.

I sit next to Siren.

Nora pokes her head in. "I'm going to try and get some sleep. If you need a break, wake me up, and I can sit with her."

"I won't need a break," I say, staring at a sleeping Siren.

Nora smiles. "I know. Wake me up if there is any change."

"I will."

Nora leaves me in the room at the back of the plane with Siren sleeping in the bed.

I run my hand through my long hair.

"I'm wearing my hair down for you. I know you like it better this way. Open your eyes and see for yourself," I say.

But of course, she doesn't open her eyes.

I sigh.

"This plane is huge, and we have a bed all to ourselves. We could really do some damage to our mile-high status on this plane," I joke.

Nothing.

"Yea, okay, that was dumb."

Just be with her.

Maybe words aren't the way.

I grab her hand, planning on holding it until she wakes up. There's a shock, probably static electricity. I pull my hand back for a second, and her eyes open.

"My anchor," she sighs.

"Yes, I'm your anchor," I say, still not knowing why she calls me that.

I reach out to pull her into a hug at the same time she sits up, but there's that damn static electricity again, shocking us both. It seems to hurt Siren worse than it does me.

"I'm sorry," I say, holding my hands wide and letting her come to me. I don't feel anything when she touches me, but it's clear she feels something painful.

"Never mind, I can hug you in a minute. Do you need anything? Water? Food?"

She shakes her head, smiling. "Just you."

I nod. "You have me."

"My anchor," she says again with a bigger smile on her face. "You've been my anchor this whole time. Thank you for saving me again."

"It seems like you did a pretty good job saving yourself. I just got you the last little bit. Only minor injuries."

She nods, her smile falling a little. *Please tell me he didn't rape you.*

"He didn't rape me."

I exhale. "Thank you," I whisper.

She nods, her eyes watering. "I fell for you, Zeke. I tried not to. Every man who falls for me ends up dead."

Our eyes meet. She knows Hugo is dead. I don't know how, but she does.

I nod, though, confirming her thoughts.

"I don't want you to suffer the same fate."

"I won't."

She swallows. "You want to know when you became my anchor?"

I nod.

"When I saved you. You were weak, out of it on my boat, looking a lot like I look right now."

"No, no one is as beautiful as you." I want to touch her, but I don't want to shock her, so I'll wait until the end of her story.

She smiles. "There was a storm, choppy waves. I knew I had to get you to land as fast as possible. It was the only way you'd survive. So I pushed us faster. Harder into the waves.

"One of the waves was too big. It pushed me overboard. I tried to swim against the current, but I was too weak. You were drifting away. But, somehow, my ankle got twisted up in a rope. A rope tied to the boat. All I had to do was hold on and you pulled me back."

I stroke her face, and watch it turn to pain at my touch.

"I was far too weak to pull you back," I say.

"It didn't matter. We were tied together. When all hope was gone, you pulled me back. Maybe not intentionally, but you gave me strength. I had to save you, and you had to save me. When I got back on the boat, I felt myself falling, my heart beating for you. Call it instant love. Call it fate. I don't know. But it scared me. I needed to get away from you."

I nod.

"God, I need to kiss you."

"Then kiss me."

I do. I devour her. I need this kiss to be fucking everything.

She screams in pain as soon as my lips touch hers.

The doctors fly into the room, and I'm pushed back. Every time they touch her, she screams like she's being shocked.

What did he do to her?

Why can't she handle being touched?

And how can I love her without touching her?

39

SIREN

IT TAKES the doctors a minute to realize what happened to me. It takes Zeke and me even less time.

I remember. Bishop shocked me. He played games with my head until I hated being touched. Then he sold me to my love, knowing I couldn't handle him touching me.

He thought it would break us. It might have, if something else didn't break us first.

A truth that turned out to be a lie. A truth I found out accidentally. A truth Zeke never thought I'd learn.

The doctors fuss over me most of the plane ride. Zeke speaks to me some, but we don't try touching again. We hardly talk until I'm back at Zeke's house.

Then everything comes out.

"You lied to me," I say.

Zeke stares at me. "What?"

"You said you didn't sell those women. You said you saved them."

"I did."

"You lied."

"What are you talking about? You should rest, and we

245

can talk more in the morning. I have doctors coming who can help reverse what happened to you."

I scream. "This can't be reversed just like that! Is that all that matters to you? Touching me?"

"No, that's not what I meant. I'm just trying to help you."

I grab his hair and yank hard, needing to hurt Zeke without shocking myself.

But I'm already in pain. So much pain. Zeke isn't the man I thought he was. I have high standards for the men I love. I thought Zeke would pass my tests.

I was wrong.

"I've been falling in love with you since the moment I saved you," I say.

"And I've been falling—"

I can't hear him say it.

"I gave up everything to save you. I risked everything," I continue as my tears come.

Zeke stills at the sight of my tears and not being able to do a damn thing to help me. Not because he can't touch me, but because he's just like all the other men in my life.

This is how I get rid of him. This is how Zeke leaves my life.

I have to get through this first. Just a little longer.

"Lucy is safe. I'll make sure you know exactly where she is before I leave."

"Leave? You are in no state to go anywhere, Siren. You're not going anywhere."

But I am. There is no use fighting him on this. I need to leave. I'm not going far. Just to Julian's. To figure out how to cross out his name from my body.

"You're not going anywhere with me, Siren. I know you're free now that Hugo is dead. You no longer owe anything to Julian. Your debt is over."

If only it were that easy.

"I used to love you, you know. Until I learned that you are just like all the rest of the dangerous men in my life."

"What are you talking about, Siren?"

"The women you supposedly saved. The women you said you didn't sell. They had a different story to tell. Two of the women were sold to Bishop. They were sold by you, Zeke. You didn't save them. You sold them."

Zeke doesn't respond. He just blinks at me. "Bishop, who?"

"I don't know, but you aren't even going to deny it?"

"No, you are the only woman I care to save. I love you, Siren. I want you. And I'm the man for you."

I shake my head as he walks closer.

"I'm going to fight for you. I'm going to kill Bishop for what he did to you. I'll rescue any woman I want. I'll spill every secret, lie, and horrible thing I did in front of your feet so that you can make me pay in blood for my sins. You're the person for me, Siren. You, not Lucy. Not Kai. Not any other woman. You're mine."

God, his words are everything. But I've heard them before. From Hugo. From Julian.

I thought they would sound different coming from Zeke, but they don't. They all sound the same. Because all the men in my life are the same—murderous monsters who only care about themselves.

"You're free now, Siren. Free from Julian. Together we can take him down. Together we can find our happily ever after."

Oh god, his words are going to kill me.

But he still doesn't understand my truth. I hope to god the words he's saying aren't the truth. Because I realized one thing with my time with Bishop. I can't be with Zeke, no matter if I love him or not. Whatever his reason for lying to me about selling the women, I might be able to forgive him —maybe.

I won't allow myself. I'm better off alone.

"I'm not free."

"Yes, you are." Zeke grabs my hand, and it burns. I jerk my hand free.

He steps back sadly.

"I'm not free, Zeke. Saving Hugo wasn't the only vow I made. My ten years might be over, but I've saved others. I owe more debts."

Zeke frowns. "None of those men matter."

I shake my head. "Every life matters. Good, evil. Strong, weak. I want to save everyone. Just like I wish someone would have saved me before I became this dark version of myself."

"What are you saying, Siren?"

"I'm saying that I'll never be free of Julian, but I can be free of you. You are the one man I will never save. I used to love you. I would have done anything for you. But you proved to me that all men are evil. That all men hurt women. That you are just as vile."

I did it. I told my first lie out loud to another person. Because everything out of my mouth is lies. And everything I'm feeling is lies too. I don't feel pain when Zeke touches me. I feel nothing but love.

Bishop didn't take my love away from me. He showed me Zeke's fate if I let him fall in love with me—death. Every man who loves a siren dies, whether the siren wants them to or not.

I love Zeke. I'll always love Zeke. Zeke protected those women with everything he had. He didn't sell them. Someone else did. Someone he loved betrayed him.

He'll figure that out soon enough. But for now, this will

give us distance. He can think I hate him. That I can't touch him. That I don't love him. It's the only way to protect him.

The fight I see in Zeke's eyes scares me. I'm afraid this time, it's too late. That he can see through my lies. That this time, he's fallen in love with me. And that love will destroy him.

Run, Zeke. Run back to your friends. Only they can protect you from me.

And then I do the one thing that I know will push Zeke away from me. Hopefully, for good.

I pull out a piece of paper with Lucy's new address.

"Lucy needs you."

The lies spill effortlessly from my lips now. *Apparently, lying for love is easy.*

Zeke stares at the address before ripping it up. And then he pushes past me.

"I'll be back," he says, grabbing the keys to his truck before he leaves.

No, you won't.

So this is what real heartbreak feels like...

The End

Thank you so much for reading! Zeke and Siren's story continues in Tangled Promise #4

Grab the entire Sinful Truths series below!
Sinful Truth #1
Twisted Vow #2
Reckless Fall #3
Tangled Promise #4
Fallen Love #5
Broken Anchor #6

Read Enzo and Kai's story below in the Truth or Lies series!
(You also get to read Zeke's beginning)
Taken by Lies #1
Betrayed by Truths #2
Trapped by Lies #3
Stolen by Truths #4
Possessed by Lies #5
Consumed by Truths #6

FREE BOOKS

Read **Taken by Lies** for **FREE!** And sign up to get my latest releases, updates, and more goodies here→EllaMiles.com/freebooks

Follow me on **BookBub** to get notified of my new releases and recommendations here→Follow on BookBub Here

Join **Ella's Bellas FB group** to get **Pretend I'm Yours** for FREE→Join Ella's Bellas Here

ORDER SIGNED PAPERBACKS

I love putting my signed paperbacks on SALE!

Check them out by visiting my website:
https://ellamiles.com/signed-paperbacks

ALSO BY ELLA MILES

SINFUL TRUTHS:

Sinful Truth #1

Twisted Vow #2

Reckless Fall #3

Tangled Promise #4

Fallen Love #5

Broken Anchor #6

TRUTH OR LIES:

Taken by Lies #1

Betrayed by Truths #2

Trapped by Lies #3

Stolen by Truths #4

Possessed by Lies #5

Consumed by Truths #6

DIRTY SERIES:

Dirty Beginning

Dirty Obsession

Dirty Addiction

Dirty Revenge

Dirty: The Complete Series

ALIGNED SERIES:

Aligned: Volume 1 (Free Series Starter)

Aligned: Volume 2

Aligned: Volume 3

Aligned: Volume 4

Aligned: The Complete Series Boxset

UNFORGIVABLE SERIES:

Heart of a Thief

Heart of a Liar

Heart of a Prick

Unforgivable: The Complete Series Boxset

MAYBE, DEFINITELY SERIES:

Maybe Yes

Maybe Never

Maybe Always

Definitely Yes

Definitely No

Definitely Forever

STANDALONES:

Pretend I'm Yours

Finding Perfect

Savage Love

Too Much

Not Sorry

ABOUT THE AUTHOR

Ella Miles writes steamy romance, including everything from dark suspense romance that will leave you on the edge of your seat to contemporary romance that will leave you laughing out loud or crying. Most importantly, she wants you to feel everything her characters feel as you read.

Ella is currently living her own happily ever after near the Rocky Mountains with her high school sweetheart husband. Her heart is also taken by her goofy five year old black lab who is scared of everything, including her own shadow.

Ella is a USA Today Bestselling Author & Top 50 Bestselling Author.

Stalk Ella at:
www.ellamiles.com
ella@ellamiles.com